OF FUTURES PAST

A Novel

Julian Bound

A moment,
a respite from what has been, of what is to come.
And so, a new lifetime begins.

ABOUT THE AUTHOR

Born in the UK, Julian Bound is a documentary photographer, film maker and author. Featured on the BBC news, National Geographic and in the international press, his work focuses on the social documentary of world culture, religion and traditions, spending time studying meditation with the Buddhist monks of northern Thailand and with spiritual teachers of India's Himalaya region.

His previous work has included documenting the soldiers of the Burmese Karen National Liberation Army, the Arab spring of 2011, Cairo, Egypt, and the Thailand political uprisings of 2009 and 2014 in Bangkok.

With portraiture of His Holiness the 14th Dalai Lama, Julian has photographed the Tibetan refugee camps of Nepal and India. His other projects include the road working gypsies of India, the Dharavi slums of Mumbai, the rail track slums of Jakarta and the sulphur miners at work in the active volcanoes of eastern Java, Indonesia.

Present for the Nepal earthquakes of 2015, he documented the disaster whilst working as an emergency deployment photographer for various NGO and international embassies.

'Of Futures Past' is his fifth novel.

CONTENTS

Eventually, two souls destined to meet shall do so,
their connection instantly recognised within the eyes of another.

PROLOGUE

The Bering Strait
21,000BC

Cold pierced through his soles once more as wet leather bindings pulled tight across unsteady feet, a brief glance back onto snows travelled bringing the familiar glow of white that had chased him since dawn.

A heavy set brow not sufficient enough, he shielded his eyes with fur wrapped hand before turning from his lone trail of deep footprints, continuing onwards, each step a painful reminder of his quest.

Thoughts of those left behind came to him. Memories of warmth filled his heart on recalling the fires he knew still burnt in his homelands. It was the ones sat huddled around those fires that now warmed his sprit, giving him renewed strength to keep moving forwards on this his third day after moon fall without those who had once given such comfort.

Reaching into the crude leather bag slung over stooped shoulder accompanying his journey he fumbled inside. The last scraps of food within would last another day, the provisions of which he knew would sustain him best, a result of knowledge of the plant life of his youth and his study of the medicinal properties contained within. This gave added impetus to reach his goal, to see those wide open plains which offered abundance, the ones his forefathers had spoken of when young.

The landscape ahead signalled night's approach. Looking onto pink tinges playing across a dimming horizon he took a handful of berries from his bag. Downing all in one hurried swallow he traipsed onwards aware of the little time left before the sun's full retreat.

The noise came again. No fear came to the lonesome traveller, so used was he to the roaring crash of breaking ice flows beneath his path. These unknown sounds were now considered a welcomed intrusion, a steadfast companion on his journey eastwards to what he sought.

His pace quickened as the rumbling below subsided. Invigorated by his meagre meal he ignored the biting chill across his features and stared upwards to a falling sun.

In the last rays of daytime's heat he recalled his elder's explanations of safe haven that remained etched on the granite walls of the home in which he had grown. Each small detail stayed with him, every display of plentiful food, each hill and valley that offered so much.

Renewed determination arrived to him, sure as he was that on finding such a place he would return to his family, and so guide them in safety to this paradise revealed by an aged hand's charcoal promises.

Faces of loved ones sat beneath that ancient map joined his thoughts, recollections of those missed lit by the licks of flame of their home's fireplace. These memories brought an added torment to the physical pain now felt and he shook his feelings from him, full concentration was needed now.

Marching onwards beneath the sky's first stars his strides extended in anticipation of what was to come, remembering the sights above that had kept him distracted by nightfall's freezing temperatures. So too tonight, he resolved, he would trace his fingertips over the white band of flickering light cutting through the darkness above him.

Looking back again onto steps taken he stared out onto bleak darkening snow surrounding his solitary walk. Shades of deepening blues began to replace the familiar stark white sheen. His view returned to a distant horizon, disappointment coming in seeing its once pink framing loose its lustre in dusk's advance.

His gaze searched the landscape for shelter, a tree, a bush, something that would provide respite from the increasing winds picking up around him. As with all previous nights there was none.

Hunger burned an accustomed path to his stomach and he reached to his bag. He stopped. Aware of his mission's importance he instead took the blanket that swung next to his paltry supplies, the only other means of comfort on his arduous journey.

It was in these moments gentle fatigue took place over optimism. Misunderstood emotions plagued him now. Concerned only with the welfare of his family he battled to understand any reasoning behind his journey. The basics of the human condition returned to calm an underdeveloped mind, its capacity now pushed to the maximum. Lowering to the ground he prepared to bed down for the night.

Curling up on his side with blanket wrapped around him, his emotional abilities were stretched once more. Breathing in the scent of his mate who too had shared his now only cover, he thought of her green eyes, the ones that always brought such comfort, the ones he longed to stare into once more.

His struggle to comprehend all that had gone before closed in on him and a single tear rolled over parched cheek and jaw. A want to continue through the night pushed to the fore, but weakness hung over him now, ache of limb and soreness of foot proving too much of a hindrance to endure. Pulling the blanket closer his thoughts returned to the map that had prompted his travels through the harshest of environments.

The lines he knew by heart, each curve of rudimentary figure, every primal representation of beast and fauna. There was one element that always fascinated him and he recalled how he longed to see the large body of water represented in waved lines over rock and stone. These sketches had produced new hope within his soul, triggering a connection made in which to escape the developing ice banks threatening him and his small community.

Ideas of finding sanctuary fell from him and simple memories reverted back to a composition of browns and blacks.

He too had tried to emulate his elder's mastery of primitive strokes. A new found emotion had appeared in those times. Not understanding the concept of frustration he had continued with his drawings, unwavering in his want to achieve the joy and silent peace felt every time in doing so.

Peeking out from the furs now keeping the cold at bay, any thoughts on drawing on the walls of his new home to be of the journey now undertaken faded on seeing the display evolving above.

Fearing the outside cold as to place a finger over the celestial scene he instead pulled his knees up close to his chest and stared to the galaxies and star systems he knew nothing of.

Lost in webs of white haze pin pointed by distant suns his breathing slowed. Euphoria entered his spirit. For the first time in days the pain that had shrouded his whole body receded. Familiar aches and the sharpness of blistered skin diminished, as did the cold which had escorted each and every one of his footfalls. Howling winds ebbed away into the background leaving him in silence to watch the forming of stars from millennia ago, a time when he and his kind had yet to exist.

Curiosity entered his primitive mind. A wonder of why he no longer felt cold when all around him betrayed such moments prompted him to cast down his and his love's blanket. As the coldness continued its unexpected departure he settled into refuge found. Any further thoughts as to the reasoning behind unforeseen warmth bid farewell also.

Rapture regained its hold on his continued observation of the cosmos playing out overhead, extending his arm fully as to run a pointed finger down its intricate weave.

Pulling his arm back his customary curled body stretched outwards and he lay back to capture the display in full sight. The melodic rise and fall of his chest slowed, icy mists reducing in time from dehydrated lips.

His view eventually left that of which had brought him such delight, distracted by what the horizon now delivered. Highlighted in starlight a solitary figure now walked towards him.

A want of knowing if friend or foe approached held little importance now. Any fear which would have once been present was lost to him. Somehow he knew of what was to pass.

Watching the man step closer along snows yet to be travelled, he wondered how another could stand so straight with no characteristic posture of arched gait he was so accustomed to. Returning to the scene of shining star trails he awaited his visitor's arrival.

The creaking sound of foot on snow at his side broke him from his gaze and he turned his head to new found company.

"You have travelled far," the figure smiled.

He listened as unknown words formed before him. Finding comfort within those mysterious tones a nod came from him with what little strength remained.

"And so too have I, at your side," the figure continued. "Now it is time for another journey."

A light of pure brilliance extended from around the figure's body, melding with the glow of hidden stars dissecting the skies above them both.

Raising his arm towards the figure, any fear, frustration or worry left his thoughts. In reassurance the figure took his hand in his, and then, they were gone.

CHAPTER ONE

Midtown Manhattan
New York City, USA
Present day

She wanted to look back, to stare once more into the eyes of a stranger, the ones that had captivated her from their first moments together.

Caught within the city's morning rush any hope of a return to her surprise encounter faded. Joining the masses walking to their desired destination she held her coffee cup to her, its warmth bringing some comfort in leaving behind the one she somehow knew.

Beneath clear blue autumnal skies she jostled for position amid a crowded side walk, her thoughts swimming with her chance meeting only minutes earlier.

It had been a full six months since her arrival in New York, its sprawling metropolis so different for the Californian beach fronts of which she had grown. Spending her twenty-sixth birthday just two weeks ago away from those Pacific waters she had begun to question her reasons for staying. Maybe now she had found one.

Both friends and family had spoken of the same encouragement, of how her new home may better suit the tenacious and sassy qualities held, so unlike that of the laidback sometimes melancholy of west coast living. An opportunity not be missed she would tell herself. A dream job.

Fresh out of art school her pursuits in oils could have seen her to a successful career as an artist, yet her true passions had always directed her towards the work of others from centuries past. Of the reasons for her want to be amongst these old masters of the arts she could never put into words the affinity met with when in the presence of such varying artworks.

Pushing onwards through the crowds her mind wandered to the paintings awaiting her touch, the ones she now spent her working days amongst, delicately restoring images of oil on wood or canvas within the depths of the city's finest art gallery.

It was always an honour to be so close to these pieces. These snapshots of eras past had been the reason behind her remaining in the city so unlike the sunshine and beaches of her formative years, although now it seemed, there was another.

She pulled her coat close to her to ward off the cold she had always abhorred and breaking free of commuters lost in early morning haste entered the park of woodland area, its gentle curved paths leading to her studio and the delights contained within. Her pace slowing, she took the last sip of coffee and revelled in the moments that had followed its purchase.

In her time in New York the world of dating had played little on her mind. So content within the confines of her work, the few dates she had been cajoled into taking by her fellow workmates had left a questioning of if she really wanted to spend her lifetime with another.

Always considering that the comfort found in art had always satisfied her emotional needs, such notions were dismissed that morning in the moment she had looked to the one who had held the coffee shop door open for her exit.

A brief exchange of thank you accompanied by a blush from each had sealed their fate it seemed. Without thought she had accepted his offer of dinner that evening, desperately trying to listen and remember where and when they would meet as she fell further into his mesmerising green eyes and the golden flecks that danced within them.

On entering her place of work a lightness of step that had been missing for so long came, as did a similar lightness fall upon her shoulders.

She gave a smile to the white bearded security guard who would welcome her each morning on walking into the gallery, a greeting it seemed only she was party to, all around her it seemed that no-one gave those of lesser standing the time of day. This went against her principles, an internal understanding always carried that everyone is equal and so deserves the same respect be they peers or underlings.

Going down the stairs leading to the basement level and along the corridors leading to her studio, memories of her encounter that morning accompanied her footsteps, most notably the kindness discovered in the eyes of a stranger. Aware her wants to know all about him would come soon enough that evening, she fought to return her mind back onto the day's work ahead. An open doorway brought her back into the present.

Taking the short passageway off the gallery's main underground thoroughfare she glanced to her studio at its end and then to the door at her side. Trying to ignore its strange pull beckoning her to enter, her need to see what lay within overrode all reasoning. With a cautious step she entered the room and looked to the treasures held within.

Greeted with the large tapestry hung across the back wall of the room, she closed her eyes for a moment and breathed in the enticing scents of centuries past. Intoxicated by the dust filled histories these woven stitches portrayed she edged closer, her eyes wide in examination of the intricate craftsmanship from another era.

Representations of a family of noble stock stared back at her beneath areas of blue sky which had been first to be meticulously cleaned by a skilled hand. Dour faces still hidden behind centuries old grime continued their glare, waiting to be released from their layers of dust and after effects of a lifetime spent in candle light.

Stepping back to take the whole tapestry in view her training emerged on identifying the details of which this artefact belonged. Although it was not her specific area of expertise as her joy remained in the restoration of aged old oils, her knowledge came to the fore on determining a date and location for the piece, only to be confirmed by the hand written notes beside the eighth century tapestry that had travelled across the Atlantic from England's northern reaches to be lovingly restored.

Her curiosity satisfied she made to leave the studio only to come to a halt at its door. Once more pulled to artwork from the hand of a soul departed from this world hundreds of years ago she crouched down, a want burning inside to pick up the knight's shield before her, to touch its flamboyant display of black feathers painted in orderly fashion across what had once been a background of white.

Standing up and looking to the details next to the battle worn piece her assumptions of early twelfth century ran true although she stumbled on its origins. Northern France had crossed her mind but only with fleeting grace, so sure was she that the shield had found a home in many countries during its trek across the tips of North Africa, its noble quest to arrive at the steps of Jerusalem.

Ideas of knights and their journeys led onto thoughts of the one met with only one hour ago. Making for her own studio she raised a smile to memories of the chivalry shown to her that morning, coupled with those green eyes she could not forget as their owner had held the door wide open for her.

Beneath her studio's doorframe she looked to the three pieces that would see her through the weeks ahead. Taking off her coat she prepared for her day in the windowless room that retained its brightness from the collection of classical artworks pinned across its walls, each of which had graced the studio table at which she now sat.

With a flick of a switch the table top illuminated, its intensity was soon dimmed in provision for the first of the morning's pieces to be restored.

Her decision to work on three pieces at one time proved to be a good one. Not only did it allow each artwork some breathing time between extensive cleaning and retouching, it also gave its restorer the ability to keep fresh in her work, and so never tiring of what lay before her.

Dimming the light a little more due to the age of the open book now at her fingertips she looked to the small rectangular box in the upper left hand corner of its right hand page, examining the ornate designed capital letter contained within. Its slight curl of tip and tail portrayed an artistic soul to her, yet there remained a sense of entrapment about the beginning letter of religious prose from the Italian libraries of Florence's Basilica di Santa Croce.

Preparing the chemical concoctions to bring back the once vibrant colours from near on seven centuries earlier her thoughts remained with its artist, her empathy surrounded by the wants of what seemed a creative soul confined to the orders and instructions of bygone religious fervour.

Becoming lost within her work two hours soon passed, each gentle touch of soft sponge against areas of sanctified parable revealing vivid pigments held within. Leaning back in her seat she glanced to the next of the three pieces that claimed her time and skills.

More suited to her area of knowledge, the two Asian artworks stood side by on easels overlooking the table which would soon become a temporary home to them also.

Replacing the book worked on that morning back on its stand she studied the two remaining artworks before reaching for the one that would see her through until lunch time.

Dismissing the returning thoughts of her morning encounter and eventual meeting over dinner to come that night, she placed the canvas awaiting her attention onto the table and spent a moment to take in its beauty.

Although the piece remained unfinished its fame had grown for that exact reason. She had always held a fascination towards the mid-seventeenth century artist from southern Japan, and her smiles that morning came from the realisation that the canvas before her now was in her presence, alone and without the distraction of other viewers, as was the case with all artworks which had gained such a famous reputation be it from academics or layman.

There had been some trepidation on being given the canvas to clean. This worry lay not in her abilities to restore the slight fading of colours, but of the desire to complete what the artist had set out to depict.

Much like another artist's famous rendition of a hidden smile, legend had surrounded the canvas before her now and she wondered if the famed Japanese painter of koi carp had intentionally left only a wash of tranquil pond and its curved shape of koi on her canvas, or was it true that she had met with her last moments during the creation of such beauty.

It mattered little to the reasoning behind the intrigue held in myth, the said beauty had remained for close to four hundred years now. All that played on the young restorer's mind now was the want to continue what the artist had wanted to achieve, to etch out the delicate lines of fin and scale and so complete the painting.

Pushing such ideas from her, she raised another smile to the thought of the repercussions to such actions. Maybe then she would have had to enter the other career she had once considered, the one that had been cast aside in her wanton passion for artistic pursuits.

Leaning back in her chair she shook the thoughts racing within her now. Closing her eyes she paid attention to her body as it inhaled and exhaled in drawn out breathes and so calming her whole being.

The technique of relaxing her often racing mind had come to her at an early age when as a child she had become enthralled by the burgundy robe wearing monks of snow-capped mountain peaks depicted in a found photography magazine. From that day she had decided upon learning all she could about them and their ways. Meditation came as a result of her curiosity, a saving grace for the inquisitive and tenacious mind she and others around her knew she held.

With eyes open, her body calmed, she looked to the third artwork awaiting her touch, the piece saved for the afternoon, when she would fall under the spell of the artwork produced by the very hands of the burgundy robed men of Tibet whose beliefs and practices aided her existence.

Turning from the bright coloured Tibetan painting she returned her view to the priceless uncompleted work from feudal Japan set out before her. Honing her focus onto the task at hand and pushing all other thoughts from her, she began to clean the canvas' peaceful waters and its inhabitant she longed to give life to.

As with the restoring of religious calligraphy that morning the hours flew by once more, the only sign of time passing revealed in the slight growl of stomach signifying lunch time's approach.

Setting the Japanese canvas aside and reaching for her coat she walked to the door only to pause before the Tibetan thangka painting that would greet her return. Taking a moment to study the piece she looked to the blue skies and the blue bird flying within them above a scene from Buddhist scripture and legend.

A want to stay and begin the repair needed to return the piece to its former splendour played on her heart, the stories surrounding the artwork pulling on romantic sensibilities. Her pause turned into minutes and would have proceeded into the full hour of her lunch break had she not torn herself away from her studio.

Leaving the gallery grounds her thoughts remained on the Tibetan monk who had painted the canvas awaiting her return. The tales of intrigue of how it had taken him close to thirty years to complete encircled the thangka master's final painting. It was these stories that enticed her to continue with her chosen career, her determination showing in that she may uncover the mystery as to what the significance of the thangka's blue bird held, the painting of less than half a century ago being the only Tibetan artwork to display such a creature so prominently.

Aware of the need to clear her thoughts, the young restorer decided on spending her given time away from the bustling coffee shops she would often frequent. Today her chosen stroll through New York's greatest of wide open spaces appeased her wants, providing the same peace and serenity found when alone with some of the world's most precious artworks.

She fell into the same routine that had calmed her soul earlier, her breathing slowing and beginning to match her gradual footfalls between pathways lined with trees of orange and reds.

Those autumnal branches arching above her walk brought an added stillness to her thoughts. Gazing up to leaves that in weeks would cover the walkways now taken her heart settled, giving rushing ideas and notions space to be aired.

Memories of the brief encounter that had led to her dinner date that evening came to her first, yet there were other thoughts lurking within her, calling out for her attention. Searching within she at last found what was causing slight unsettlement, albeit confined to the far reaches of her subconscious.

She had brushed over what was in need of being confronted only hours ago and was now aware it was time to work through the thoughts that at times hounded her so.

Looking to the green lawns and the gentle slopes pin pricked with the occasional premature yellowing leaf, she recalled her thoughts that morning on the other career she at one time had considered. Had it not been for the love held for the art that invigorated her emotions so well, she was sure she would have aimed such devotion into the life of a doctor.

Medical practices had always held her in great enthrallment, both in fields of modern day and alternative medicines. Each to her served a purpose, beliefs confirmed in the charting of centuries gone by, theoretical studies that were now beginning to be deliberated throughout the medical journals she would pour over from time to time, a guilty pleasure held onto dearly.

When the thought of a life within medicine at times hounded her soul, it would often only lead to confirm her chosen path amid works of humankind's greatest artists, always deciding this was what she was doing this lifetime, an assurance in her words bringing awareness that maybe the life of doctor was resigned to her next.

Ease of mind came in these solutions of slight torment on turning back towards the gallery, intent on returning to the Tibetan painting, the composition of which portrayed a soul's journey through many lifetimes.

Continuing in mindfulness beneath the same clear sky that had greeted her that morning she soon found herself nodding hello to the gallery security guard once more. Passing by him she made for her studio only to come to stop again outside an open door.

A look to either side of her and then in the direction of her own studio gave her the courage to enter the door standing slightly ajar before her.

Entering the studio with some apprehension, knowing it was out of bounds to someone on her pay scale, she could not resist what was contained within the domain of her peers.

Squinting through the dim light needed to protect the two treasures now standing before her, she waited for her eyes to adjust before taking in the first of the artworks she had studied in books since her early days of art school.

On stepping back as to take in the whole canvas her eyes scanned over every brush mark applied in what seemed an explosion of controlled frenzy, making out its composition of three figures in various dancing poses, aware of the importance of the canvas of such unconventional beauty and how it had changed the course of world art in the heady days of northern Paris, and its artistic temperaments that resided upon its quarter's cobbled streets.

Aware of the soon return of those working on the cleaning of the higher echelons of artistic endeavours her gaze left the Spanish artist's towering painted depiction of supposed love triangle and fell to the painting that captivated her heart on each viewing made.

Not understanding why the pull of the Italian artist's representation of a young woman played so strong on her, she stared at the in fine lines of umber oils on a backdrop of light ochre.

With a professional eye her view ran across delicate cheekbones and pensive stare of the artists' model. It was she that had always drawn the young restorer to the piece. It was her gaze that gave such fascination, framed by locks of curls left uncompleted in the style of early sixteenth century courtesans.

She longed to reach out and hold the small wooden panel which had cast a spell over her senses. To feel its weight play across her palms, to be as close to the painting as could be and so sating both physical and emotional needs.

In her internal battle she thought of the one she had met with on her way to work and how as with the artwork now in front of her, she had wanted to reach out and hold him also.

As memories of the green eyes encountered returned she stumbled backwards against the studio's wall. Her view still on the centuries old portrait she raised a hand to her chest in want of making the searing pain within her body stop. All attempts failed. As her knees buckled beneath her she slid downwards until sitting crouched on the floor, her back pressed against the wall.

The pain continued, yet no fear entered her soul. Staring at the portrait she tried to focus on her breathing that had now collapsed into the shallowest of breaths. Closing her eyes she tried to inhale and exhale in peaceful rhythm, the way she had always done so in times of stress. With each breath her pain subsided until its sharp surprise had completely gone.

Opening her eyes she looked to the figure standing above her. Watching him crouch down to her she looked into the kind blue eyes that greeted her now. Part of her knew she had seen them so many times before, although in her brief realisations of such moments she was unable to hide her regret.

The man smiled on taking her hand in his.

"It is time," he said.

She gave a nod of understanding to him, but still disappointment hung upon her.

"And so shall you one day look into those green eyes again," the man reassured her thoughts as a white glow began to fill the room.

Feeling comfort in his words, the young restorer watched the light flow over the two paintings she had always felt such affinity for, and looking to the one she felt she had always known her fingers wrapped around his as both became shrouded in pure white light.

CHAPTER TWO

Looking to her feet as white light faded around her, fine grained sands now replaced the carpeted flooring of New York gallery.

No panic came in the discovery of her new setting on gazing out before her onto a view of calm seas where treasured artworks had stood only moments before.

Listening to the gentle lap of waves and feeling soft warm breezes flow across her brow she smiled out onto a distant horizon and then to the man beside her, his hand still held in hers.

"Isn't it beautiful," he said, his words as much statement as question.

Giving a simple nod to his words her eyes returned to where sky met with sea, watching soft clouds drift over vibrant green and blue waters as fingernails of white surf caught in amber sunlight appeared brief and fleeting across the scene. Never before had she seen such a sight.

"It is," she whispered.

Her soul enriched with the peace now surrounding her, she turned to her companion.

He knew of the words she would now speak. The question he had heard her ask so many times before.

"Where am I?" Those words at last came.

Releasing her hand he too looked out onto the seas that captivated her so, preparing his reply, aware that each encounter with the one who stood with him now always required a different approach in ways of explanation.

"How did I get here?" She said to him. "And who are you?"

Turning from the sea view he smiled to her questioning.

"All will become apparent," he told her. "Come, let us walk awhile."

Stepping from her he walked besides where sea met with shale.

"My name is George," he called back to her, continuing onwards, awaiting her arrival.

She watched him walk from her and looked to her surroundings.

Leaving the pull of tranquil seascape her view carried from the endless beachfront George now walked and came to rest on the low cliff edge running parallel with beach and lapping waves.

A tall two story building sat on the cliff's edge its wooden frontage, high gothic style windows and rooftop watching over the beach she had found herself upon.

Her attention fell to the lone bush set aside from the building, its leafless branches sharp and angled, containing what seemed an endless collection of thorn and twig.

Drawn towards bush and building, a want to take the small winding pathway that would lead her to both called for her footsteps.

"We will soon be visiting there," George called out to her.

Reassured by his words, she stared up to the wooden structure so reminiscent of the solitary early twentieth century artworks she had always enjoyed and then caught up with the man who it seemed knew her so well.

"Here she is," he said on her arrival at his side.

Feeling a once unknown comfort her footfalls fell in line with his and she looked out onto the horizon once more.

"How can this be possible?" She asked.

"How can what be possible?"

"Well, this," her outstretched arm swept across all before them. "Am I dreaming?"

"No, this is no dream."

"Then when will I be returning to my studio?"

His pause caused her to come to a halt and she glanced up to the cliff edge building. Somehow she knew her solutions lay within its walls.

George followed her view.

"Yes," he said, "your answers lay beneath that rooftop, but first there is something that you must understand. Something that you must accept," he added before walking from her once more.

"What must I understand?" Her footsteps joined his again. "What must I accept…?" Her words trailed from her as the realisation of her situation came to the fore.

George looked to her. It was always this way, or at least had been for the last few centuries. Her understanding of what had passed coming sooner with each lifetime lived.

"Your studio, your home, all that you once identified as you has gone now," he said, his tone gentle as to provide the security he knew necessary now.

"Gone," she whispered, lost in thought, her understanding ebbing and flowing from her, much as the shallow waves at her feet now did also.

"Many times we have walked along this beach together. Many times have I watched your awareness to the reasons for your presence here emerge."

"I remember those times," she said, her voice as distant as the evading memories she now spoke of, trying to capture them again and again before they fell from her.

"All will become clear," he pointed to the cliffside building he knew pulled on her so.

Joining his view her mind explored the possibilities presented to her on the tranquil seafront she now stood. Looking to George standing beside her she began to remember the kind eyes blue eyes that looked to her now.

"Yes," George nodded once more. "You are beginning to recognise me."

"I am, but from where I don't know."

Continuing his gaze upon her, George knew she was ready to hear his words now, that her understanding would soon be reached.

"From between each lifetime spent," came his answer, his hand reaching into hers once more.

Taking his welcoming palm and wrapping her fingers soft against his, as with her slow recognition held within his blue eyes remembrances of past moments filtered into her consciousness. This aided her understanding that her lifetime spent formerly beside Californian Pacific waters then later in her homeland's fast paced metropolis had come to an end. No remorse came in the recognition that all she had known in those brief twenty-six years had gone. George's words entered her heart again as she came to accept that this is how things are.

George gave her hand a gentle squeeze in recognition and reassurance of her fresh understanding. This prompted her to look up to him, yet there was one thing she carried with her from recent past moments and her features were unable to hide her disappointment in not meeting with the one of startling green eyes.

"Who says you won't again?" George gave her hand another squeeze.

"You mean..." her words fell from her as another fleeting glimpse of what would come to pass appeared and was gone as soon as she had grasped its context.

"Many times have you met before and so shall you once again," George told her.

Seeing she was beginning to acknowledge her situation he released her hand and pointed to the bush standing pride of place besides the building they would soon enter.

"Shall we?" He asked, his arm extended out in motioning her to lead the way.

The path ahead winding up to the cliff's summit called to her once more and with a hesitant step she led George away from lapping green and blue waters.

Climbing slow and steady, the path's mild embankments gave some ease to their ascent and no time at all they both stood together looking onto the seascape spread out before them.

"Such beauty," she said, her view flowing over every aspect of the vista.

"Of that it is," George agreed, aware of the inquisitiveness growing inside her. That curiosity soon surfaced as she left the view of the beginnings of sunset.

Leaving the building pinks and reds signalling the approach of dusk she glanced to the bush now standing behind them. Both she and George turned their back to sea and sand. For as far as the eye could see the remnants of a hot summer's bracken swayed slight in cooling breezes giving the appearance of an ocean of brown and ochre. George pointed to the bush and its myriad of branch and stick.

"Can you see what this bush represents?" He asked.

Looking to the multitude of sharp twists and turns each offshoot of twig and stem made she searched within her heart. Aware it lay there somewhere within she closed her eyes, determined to find an answer.

"Open your eyes," George whispered to her.

In doing so she gasped to what now stood before her.

What had once been barren dark twists and turns began to glow as a faint radiance flowed from the bush's small trunk and to the outer edges of each thicketed stick, bringing the whole bush to life as a small flower bud started its march towards full bloom at the end of each twig like artery.

"Pathways," she said, her sight still fixed on the expanding beauty the now displayed.

"Pathways to where?"

"These twists and entwining branches, no matter how small, are all the choices made in one lifetime," she replied, her knowledge flowing as did the pink blossoms now appearing before her. "Each flower the result of a lifetime lived," she added, new understandings coming within her words.

"Yes," George smiled. "So many decisions are made in one lifetime, each choice bringing new twists and turns to an individual's life path."

"But there are so many lifetimes."

"And who do you think they all belong to?"

Studying the bush as it became devoured in an explosion of pink and white petals her eyes widened to the answer found within her heart.

"These are all mine?"

George nodded to her.

"But they can't all be mine."

"And why not?"

"Because…" her words did not come, so in awe of living so many times before.

"Would you like to see these lifetimes you have lived through?" George nodded to the building beside them.

Staring from the flowering bush and to the building's grey and green painted wooden slat walls her curiosity peeked once more.

"Good," George beckoned her to join his walk towards the building's front doors. "Now you have accepted that this is where you are supposed to be, then so are you ready to look to the lives you have already led."

Wanting to experience all presented to her, she quickly joined George's side and together they entered into the cliffside building and all its secrets held within.

Amber sunbeams tinged with the pink edging of a dwindling sunset flowed from tall windows onto the flooring of the single roomed building, illuminating the large table sat in the center of a long aisle.

George looked to the one he had brought here many times before, delighting as he would on each occasion to the wonderment the building always produced in the soul beside him.

Aware of George's eyes upon her, she continued to gaze across the huge room, her marvel increasing on seeing the multitude of bookshelves filled to the brim lining each wall from floor to ceiling.

"So many books," she said.

"Yes," George caught her words. "Can you see yours?"

"My what? Book?"

"Why of course," George smiled to her.

Taking a seat at one of the tables two chairs he pointed to section of bookshelves beneath the large windows at the far end of the room.

Leaving George's side she walked down the aisle and to the bookshelf she had been guided towards. She came to a stop and looked to the book that now called out to her senses to reach for, its spine emitting a slight glow, increasing her need to hold it in her hands.

Remaining seated, George called out to the soul he had known for centuries.

"Bring the book to me," he said, "so we may both discover what lies within its many pages."

Reaching forwards as instructed the book's constant glow increased on her touch and she received its comfort in the form of heat flowing through her hands.

Clutching its leather bound covers to her chest she walked to George, her body bathed in a warmth that brought both comfort and wellbeing to her with every footstep.

"Here she is again," George welcomed on her approach. "Now, place the book here before us," he patted the table's rich mahogany top.

In doing so she took the seat next to George's and looked around her once more.

17

"It is quite magnificent don't you think," he said.

A single nod came from her coupled with a frown.

"And what bothers you so?" George asked.

"This is my book?"

"Yes."

"Then who do all the other books belong to?"

"That will be revealed all in good time," George positioned the lone book before her. "Now, do you know what this book, your book, contains?"

Thinking of the bush she had watched flower outside her hands placed onto the book's still warm cover. Her eyes looked into George's, his bright blue stares back to her confirming her answer.

"Yes," he knew her thoughts, "it is true. Each chapter found between these covers is a detailed account of each lifetime you have ever lived."

"And I can read them?"

"Why of course," George smiled to her. "That is, if you really want to see what has gone before?"

Watching his words take effect, he knew the tenacity and curiosity that burned within the soul seated beside him now, traits he had watched accompany her true spirit throughout each lifetime, unyielding characteristics spurring her onwards through lives lived in different eras, continents and countries.

"So this is me?"

"The essence of you."

"The essence?"

"It is who you are, what you represent, the factors that make your soul as unique and as individual as any other's."

"Then I am not always me?"

"You are always you. You are always your true self. The core of who you are, how you interact with others as well as yourself remains constant throughout, yet there are some factors that are different."

"I don't always look the same?"

"No," he smiled to her. "You do not always look the same, nor are you always in the same location."

"You mean," she paused, her mind exploring the implications George talked of now and stared back at him. "You mean that sometimes I'm a man?"

"Yes, how else could you experience life from each and every situation presented in a world filled with sentiments and emotions."

Intrigued by the connotations of what George spoke of now she reached again for her book, this time opening its cover to reveal what lay within its pages.

The slight glow that had helped her locate its position amid all other books present continued across each page now flicked through. Looking over the black type face she closed its cover and looked to George.

"I suppose I should start at the beginning," she said.

"You can start where you want," he told her. "You can delve into each chapter at will, skipping from century to century, back and forth through time. It is up to you and you alone. But," he looked to her. "Sometimes it is good to follow the natural order of things. Then you can see the progression your soul has taken from the very beginning."

Staring down at the book she considered her plan of action.

With a brief glance to the books surrounding her and George she opened the leather bound cover once more, turned to its first page and began to read.

George settled back in his chair as he watched the one beside him lose herself within the words presented before her.

Knowing of what she now read, he too recalled the barren white landscape that had seen to her first lifetime, a lifetime which had displayed a tenacity of spirit in the long hike taken across uncharted territories in freezing temperatures. He also remembered how he had found the soul he had accompanied through time, alone and ready for his arrival beneath an array of twinkling star systems.

Waiting for her to finish the prologue to her journey through the centuries he settled back in his chair once again, looking to the tall windows above them and the sunset displayed within its frame.

"That was me?"

George looked to the tear filled eyes before him. His hand reached for hers.

"Yes, it was. But can you not see that even from the very beginning, your soul portrayed a nobility and resolve that has kept with you ever since those days?"

"But he, I," she corrected, "I was alone."

"I was there with you was I not," George gave her hand a gentle squeeze.

"You were," she whispered in her reassurance. "But, I still died."

"Every story has an end, a closing of chapters that can and only lead towards the opening of a new one, a new story in either a present life lived or that of a completely new one."

Her understanding reached knew levels on beginning to foresee what was to be revealed to her.

"Now you are ready," George told her. "Now you are ready to read of the other lifetimes you have lived."

"And you will be here with me as I do so?"

"Yes," George released her hand. "I will be here at your side as I have always been."

"Always?"

"From each of your first breathes until your last ones in every lifetime, my hand held in yours on each occasion."

The comfort found in his words diminished any sadness held in reading of a cold demise upon an endless snow and ice landscape many thousands of years ago.

Warmed once more by the touch of the book of secrets before her, she turned a page and began to read of another lifetime spent, her curiosity running free in the knowledge of George's eternal presence beside her.

"England, 793AD," she whispered, intrigued by the chapter's opening words of location and date.

CHAPTER THREE

Bamburgh Castle
England
793AD

Shadows lost in midday sun, pristine lawns gave a display of rich green but for the gradual browning edges telling of June's much awaited arrival.

Summer always brought delight to the old woman of Bamburgh Castle. After months of what seemed perpetual winter, to feel warm rays across her features had always been one of her secret pleasures.

This was not her only reason for welcoming these cherished hot months. On walking from her quarters across castle courtyard and garden her thoughts filled with the bountiful harvest soon to be reaped.

Now in her seventy-fourth year it would be those select few who followed in her footsteps of chosen profession that would be entering the western woodlands, collecting precious berries and mushrooms needed for her county famed medicines and treatments.

Pausing at her home's eastern walls, the old woman took in another secret joy, the sea. Such a sight always caused a catch of breath. Since young her heart belonged to this body of water now laid out before her.

Gentle waves flowed back and to over sand and shale, bringing forth the prized seaweeds which would also become a part of her medicinal retinue.

These now tranquil waters she knew could change at any moment. Memories of vast tempests witnessed brought with them a wry smile. Much like herself she considered, even though at times her feistiness had to be tempered when in the company of those of Bamburgh's exclusive heritage.

Looking from the seas which held such fascination the old woman cast her view to the settlements below.

As with most castles of the land, communities of the poor gathered beneath tall walls of grey stone, engulfing areas once deemed desolate. It was this sight below which now produced a film of tears across aged eyes.

Remembrances revisited her of when young amid those who fought for scraps of unwanted food thrown from towering balconies. This always shaped the gratitude held within having led a life spent in comfort, that she, a girl of such humble beginnings should have been taken into the fold of those above who had plenty. Breaking free from her memories, the sea and those of her own kind, the old woman continued her path towards those who now needed her skills.

Accompanying her footfalls that day her thoughts returned to youthful times and the one act of kindness that had led the way to a life spent.

Although slightly clouded in memory its main points remained clear. The sight of the sick before six year old eyes, the choosing of whom to give her prized corner of bread to, and her choice that seemed so natural at the time to be seen by a castle elder. A simple case of destiny at play, she had always reassured her questioning on such matters, or just a thing of chance. Yet, that special day had given not only she but others also so much, leaving the old woman eternally grateful to the Bamburgh family, of which until this day she had always remained loyal.

Focused on her day ahead, the old woman put aside thoughts of the past and made for the rooms in which she had spent most of her adult life. She knew of what to expect. Those of sickness outweighing those of health in recent times, even though a portion of the ones who paid her a visit were just in need of validation of their malady.

This would often infuriate her. A waste of precious time when others of more need could be treated. It seemed the way for nobility to be a constant in her surgery, this she often put down to an idol mind, a state of being where even with all the riches a person could ask for confirmation of being was needed. The old woman's poverty stricken start in life would often shine through in those moments, wondering how the soul before her complaining of minor aches and pains while dressed in clothes of such finery would have coped, had they been born a few floors lower than the stately bedrooms in which they now slept.

Slight apprehension to the day ahead came to her. It was not the thought of sitting with blue blood's imaginary ailments that gave rise to trepidation, it was in the mood she now carried and she glanced over to her beloved sea, once more reminded of the tempestuous nature both shared.

Greeted with nods and hellos on each twist and turn within the Bamburgh Castle's inner bowls, the old woman welcomed each with a similar respect. Those who gave their cheer she knew well having delivered most into the world. The delivery of fresh souls had proved enough in life for her. For although she had no children of her own, those around proved to be more so than she imagined.

There had been suitors in her younger days. Far and wide they had travelled to see the beauty talked of across England's northern reaches, and to witness first-hand the treatments of great doctoring wrapped in the kindness rarely found among physicians of the day.

None had enticed her into a life of marriage. Those offers would have not only taken her from the work she saw as a vocation, but also from the seas of her belonging.

Arriving to the staircase leading to her clinic the old woman stopped. Breathing slowly she hoped her actions would calm the fire of emotions building within. Knowing the smallest of spark could ignite a torrent of words which in time would be regretted, she inhaled again, exhaling slowly on taking the final steps towards the day's work that lay ahead.

A nod from her cohorts already treating recent arrivals she took her place beside them and summoned the first of her patients that day.

It had been through hard work and persistence of mind that had earned her the right of starting her treatments after midday. Such was a privilege amongst others, yet they all knew this right was more than hard earned. Tales of fearless runs into battlefields stained deep with red and calls of the fallen surrounded the old woman, with the knowledge of a feisty heart giving a reign of silence over those who may oppose the work ethics of Bamburgh's celebrated doctor.

The joy of healing never escaped her. High in demand, the old woman's services provided great esteem towards the castle she called home, a respect noted by those whose crest flew above all within its walls.

Adding to the peace contained within the castle, calmness prevailed across Bamburgh's surrounding area. This, the Bamburgh gentry knew was partly due to their prized doctor playing a role in amity found. With this in mind those of royal stock turned a blind eye towards the old woman's eccentricities as they like to call it, when, in clashes with warring neighbours, she would aid those classed as enemy. It seemed peculiar that their prodigious asset should not disassociate friend from foe when it came to treating the wounded. Putting this down to the poverty experienced in her formative years no word of treason graced the lips of those in power.

Sounds of hurried footsteps on worn slate staircase brought a silence to the clinic. Each person present looked to the old woman, a want of guidance in their stares.

Taking the lead and reassuring all with a glance she stood, ready to greet who now entered her domain.

The news given by armour clad visitors confirmed the old woman's fears. Aware of the circle of life which moved back and thro with the tides of her beloved sea, she knew the peace that had held sway for many years on these north eastern shores was just a respite for what was to come.

Talk of a want for trade routes by those from colder climes far across the seas from England had been rife amid coastal townships far and wide. Each council and private chamber had refused such passage when asked or at time demanded for, now it appeared matters of want had been taken in forms of force, beginning with the holy island but a half hour on horseback from Bamburgh's standings.

Following the messengers up into daylight, the old woman calculated what would be needed in terms of cloth bandage and balm. A pioneer of healing wounds both deep and shallow, rolls of thread and sharp needle were added to the itinerary.

Slow of pace, the old woman reached the outside world at last. Finding room amongst a crush of observers she looked northwards across beige sands to the preludes of battle.

Her eyesight still strong after all these years, she too stared out onto a fleet of ships, ominous and foreboding, huge sails billowing over sterns fashioned in wooden visions of mythical creature.

A turn to her aids prompted her mental list to be given. Watching her protégés rush from her across the courtyard to retrieve items requested the old woman spied another's approach and with a customary curtsy she hid her concerns towards the harsh looks encountered from Bamburgh's lord.

Biting of tongue and a holding of temper ensued, ending with a turn of heel and spirited march back to her clinic.

Those below getting the old woman's supplies knew of their peer's advance, and of the rage contained in each footfall now echoing throughout the stairway leading to them.

On her arrival the explanation of her master's denial for her to help those in need poured from her. An added fury blazed in whispered statements of how those blocking her want of aid should well remember that it had been her features that they had first seen when entering this world, for she had delivered each and every one of them.

Not a person dared utter a single word, all present falling into the silence accompanying the old woman's pause.

Her smiles soon returned and she nodded to the large tapestry hung over the clinic's far wall.

With help she pulled back the dusty, intricately stitched portrayal of long parted aristocracy, hidden in recesses of darkened corners as was often the way. Even those of noble birth right had their skeletons of misdemeanours, often more than most.

Coughs resulting in the removal were soon replaced by gasps. All looked to the doorway that had lain hidden behind scenes of past transgressors.

With a pull by the strongest the door opened. Not a creak came, that expected sound muffled in the skills of carpenters and their adherence to orders of secrecy.

Instructions given that no one was to follow her rebellious actions the old woman began a solitary walk armed with candle light, supplies and confidence. No trepidation entered her soul on continuing through the tunnel, the one she should know little of.

Hearing the door close behind her and the ruffle of hastily replaced tapestry she walked on, each stride taken releasing her guilt. To go against those who had provided a life well spent under Bamburgh's rooftops would always be considered with thanks, but her steadfast ideals had now entered the arena. As the last of her doubts faded the old woman looked to candle lit etchings lining the passage walls she now walked between. Had she not been a doctor then she would have surely blushed.

Flickering in and out of focus, amber bathed effigies of Greek and Roman Gods joined in pleasures unknown with both Goddesses and mere mortals. These scenes were apt due to the reasoning behind such hidden passageways shrouded in secrecy, the old woman knowing all too well the fascination both Lords and Ladies held in the serving staff living at the ends of these mazes of convenience and gratification.

Turning left then right on each given occasion, the old woman found her path through the concubine's haunt and walked out of a forgotten pantry within the castle kitchens. Not one person witnessed her arrival. Certain all servants were under instruction towards commencement of confrontation, the old woman made for the stables, ready to find her mount which would carry her into battle. That worthy steed was soon found, concealed in the anonymity of empty courtyards and lawn.

Taking Bamburgh's western exit she circumnavigated her home until riding northwards along the coastal path known since a child, and the bridleway that would keep her unnoticed between avenues of prickled bush and shrub.

Anticipation and excitement revisited the old woman after many years away from times of combat.

In mind that her help was needed, she identified her own wants within the quandary of volunteering into danger.

Realisations of those needs had come at young age to the old woman, an enticement of the unexpected arriving early in her years. Now, on this beachside bridle path these same emotions visited her heart, with no difference to days of fifty years ago within the confines of mankind's joy of conflict.

A pulling of reins and steady dismount were prompted by views in the near distance. Turning her ride southwards, sure the beast knew its way homewards, the old woman's stares fell back to north eastern shores and the scene unfolding before her.

Measured steps in loose sand and warm sunlight across her brow paid little comfort towards what was now presented.

To collect her thoughts she did as she had done when young before fate had whisked her away into the inner sanctum of Bamburgh's chambers.

Beginning to inhale and exhale with slow simplicity of breath, gulls hovered above her focus, above the greens and blues of undulating sea, above the curved crescents of continual surf, and so her mind came to ease in the scene, a comfort realised in how this was where her heart lay.

Cries and yells of both pain and elation pulled her back from peace. The old woman knew what would entail having listened to battle's torment many times before. Excitement coursed through her once again. With no regrets towards her wants of affray she gathered herself and continued on her trek into as much the unexpected as the expected.

Those white crescents playing soft across tranquil waters took on a different performance. The old woman stopped once more and watched crimson tinged waves seep over her treasured beach. Looking to the display's origin she watched men, tall and strong beat down on those of slighter stature as brown robed arms flailed upwards against wielded axe and hammer.

No wince visited the old woman, her mind deflecting the true scene. A coping mechanism she suspected, for how else could she do what she did, and so well.

The blood shedding ahead quelled on her advance and her attention turned to those gathered on the beach awaiting their aggressor's arrival.

Beneath armoured suits glinting in afternoon sun, those making ready to lead looked to the old woman. She saw their displeasure in her presence. Without a care she pushed on, determined her rebellious actions would soon be justified.

A shake of head and dry smile from the one who had denied her wants confirmed her actions that day, and so she took the slight gift of approval nestling within her master's stare and made for ensuing warfare.

A collection of rock pools made for best vantage point, grey and black pock marked surfaces she was aware would soon contain soups of red. It came of little revelation when her intuitions ran true.

Screams of defiance and wrath flowed across sands sprinkled with the blood of both parties. The old woman was never surprised by the speed of a fighting man's ferocity.

Her attention drifted from the scene and once more attended the calls of green and blue waters. Knowing the hazards held in concentration's slip, the old woman broke from daydreams vulnerability. This almost proved too late.

Arriving back in the present moment she stared up to the bearded man towering above her, his arm raised, hatchet prepared to strike. Disbelief took to them both. Recollections of another's elderly feminine face read across the man's eyes. The old woman saw this and wondered of the mothers of those now attacking her home.

A slight lowering of weapon caused an imbalance in Bamburgh's unwelcomed visitor. Wet fur lined boots made for poor traction on jagged rock and he fell to the old woman's feet.

She reached for her bag on looking to the deep gash above his right eye. Kneeling before him her thoughts escaped to the one who had raised him and was sure to worry for his wellbeing.

With wound sutured tight, a squint of blood stained eye peered up at her. A time of grace filled them both, unsaid words held in clouded moments of unseen victories.

The old woman stood, hands on hips, her contempt towards the invader still present. The man rose to his feet also, staring down to her in continued distain.

Holding her look, the old woman received a simple nod before the one aided regained his footing and ran to join his compatriots.

Watching him leave the old woman stepped over predicted red filled pools. As had her antagonist done so, she too lost her balance. Grasping at air, her temple glanced off wet stone and she fell backwards into inviting waters.

The world of war faring around her dimmed. No sounds but that of animated gulls and the brush of wave entered her senses.

Floating still, shrouded in sunlight, the sea's gentle motion gave a comfort unknown. Looking upwards, she watched a lone summer's cloud find its way across blue skies, as unaware as she of the continuing fight a stone's throw away from where she now lay.

Soft laughter entered her blissful state.

"You seem to be enjoying your new position," a voice called out to her.

The old woman turned her head to the rocks which had provided entry into the elation now experienced. Looking deep into blue eyes, she gave a brief nod to the man smiling down to her and then returned her gaze upwards, her body moving as one with the seas she had always loved.

"And so this journey has come to a close," the man spoke once more. "Come, you are more than ready."

The old woman knew of what the man's words implied. She also knew she was ready, but the sensations felt now overrode her want to leave. She shook her head, prompting laughter to flow across salt waters once more.

"As tenacious as ever I see," the man said, his joy uncontained. Kneeling down he reached his hand out to the old woman.

Turning her head to him again she followed his wants and took his hand in hers.

With an aged smile, wrinkled fingers squeezed gentle around his grasp beneath a familiar light of pure white, and with a final glance up to a blue summer sky she closed her eyes.

CHAPTER FOUR

As her view left pages read, she looked to George sat patiently beside her.

"I don't know whether to laugh or to cry," she told him.

"I remember you laying there in the sea," he smiled. "You were enjoying bobbing about so much I thought you would never leave."

Looking back to the book, her mind tried to grasp that the old doctor of Bamburgh Castle had in fact been her.

George recognised her trepidation towards such ideas.

"Yes, it was you. Can you not see some traits you carry now as you did then?"

She placed her hand onto pages that retained the warmth conveyed across its leather covers, searching for the links connecting her to that of another supposed to be her, no matter how tenuous those connections may be.

Remembering the love of feeling the sun on her cheeks brought with it the first step in realisation of her soul's journey to where she now sat. This time it was she who smiled.

"The cold," she said. "It is the one thing I cannot bear."

"And why do you think that could be?" George pressed her for answers once more, guiding her thoughts with great subtly so she may discover her answers in her own time.

Memories of her book's prologue entered her heart. Recalling the sadness felt on her soul's quest to find a new home for loved ones, she began to see how her aversion to the cold may have carried forth from those last days spent within frozen northern reaches.

"Does my love for warmer weather stem from my passing amongst snow and ice?"

"This is something you have always carried with you," George nodded. "Is there anything else that can connect you to what has been? Anything that you love now as you did then?"

There was little need for her delve deep within her heart for her next answer.

"The ocean," she said, her voice distant.

"And why?"

"Was it because I never got to see it?" Her mind returned to how the one who had perished in the relentless cold had wanted to see the vast open waters which always brought her such delight.

"And was there not another who loved the water so?"

"The doctor," she giggled, picturing her floating and enjoying the gentle lift of melodic waves, much the same way she herself had experienced such joy on the warm Californian coastlines of her youth.

Thinking of from the similarities discovered now another came to her.

"She was a doctor."

"You were a doctor," George corrected.

"And I nearly was this lifetime." She paused, remembering her current situation. "Last lifetime that is."

No sadness came in the saying goodbye to that life lived, the reasons of which she could not perceive, she was just here, just where she knew she was supposed to be. George watched her brief internal struggles, mindful that the soul he had accompanied through so much always came to understand all presented.

"Yes," she whispered to herself, "I was a doctor."

George watched her acknowledgement of lives once lived flourish, yet he said nothing of this, knowing only she could provide the beliefs needed to fully understand the moments she found herself in now, in between lifetimes, a provisional respite for the soul.

"Tell me," he said, "was there anything, any object or device that you could place in the years you have lived previously?"

Thinking of the snows that had paid price to her existence thousands of years ago, her thoughts returned to the castle walls where her former self had taken the vocation to heal others. She looked to the book, longing to scour its words for the connection required. Holding back from those wants answers sought soon came.

"The tapestry," she said. "The one in the surgery that hid the doorway leading to escape. I know it. I saw it in the gallery being restored."

"Yes," George nodded, delighted she had found the link he longed her to discover. "There are many things that may seem familiar to you as we take this journey together through the pages of your book."

"And the doctor's tempestuous nature?"

"What of it?"

"Another of my traits?" She asked George, a mischievous look in her eye.

"This is true also," he laughed to her recognition and increased enjoyment to what she may uncover. "But can you see that another characteristic has been portrayed in the pages already read, a distinct quality that has carried with you from barren snowy landscapes through to northern England coastal battlements?"

She stared back down to the book reliving the two lifetimes in her mind, seeking for that of which George asked now. The cold, the healing, the love of the ocean, all these ideas came to her once more.

"A journey," she looked back to George. "They each took a journey towards the unknown."

"Yes, this is true, but think of the interactions played out in each with others."

Returning her view to the book she tried to uncover the clues in George's words. Understanding at last came to her in how the old doctor of eighth century England had helped another, devoid of being enemy of friend.

Picturing the Nordic warrior looming above her, she began to identify with the fearlessness the old doctor had portrayed. Although she may not have been in any situations that had called on such strength on the streets of New York or the calm beaches of southern California, she somehow knew that if the rise came she would have indeed acted with similar if not the exact same verve shown. Her thoughts revisited the one who had travelled across snow and ice, carving his own path into the unknown. The courage he had shown in such an act was obvious, but she knew that George waited for her to identify another trait that would adjoin herself with former selves.

George saw her struggle.

"What did they do for others?" He asked.

Prompting her answers to come forth her thinking slowed to the rush of realisations triggered by George's few words.

"The old doctor, she helped the enemy of her people. She didn't care who it was or what he had done, she just reached out to him and healed his wounds."

"Of that she did. She showed a great selflessness of character, aiding those in need, be they friend or foe."

"But what of the one who travelled away from his homelands in search of…" Her words fell from her as new understandings came.

George's blue eyes urged her to continue.

"He showed his selflessness for others by searching for a new home," she continued, "taking on the elements no matter how dangerous it was."

"And so proved the ability to put another before his own needs."

"Yes, yes they did."

She fell silent, her mind searching for such similar actions in her past life of an art restorer. None came to her.

Casting her mind back to those days now lost to her, she searched for a moment, any moment, where she had shown selflessness in her actions. Once again no such memories came to her, feeling some sorrow to the lack of such a treasured characteristic.

"It is there," George said to her. "Was there not someone you would give a moment of your time to, no matter how brief? Someone you gave your attention to when all others passed them by?"

Once more she revisited the moments that now seemed so long ago.

"There was one," she said. "The security guard at the gallery. Each morning I would say hello to him when all others didn't."

"And why would you greet him every morning when it was deemed normal not to do so?"

Something in George's words pressed her soul and she felt the fire displayed in the old doctor.

"Because it was wrong."

"What was wrong?"

"It was wrong to treat another like that. To ignore them just because they were seen to be there just to serve."

"They deserved…"

"They deserved the same respect as everybody else," she interrupted, feistiness breaking through.

Recognising her burgeoning awareness George smiled to her.

"This is what you share with the old doctor. You see it was not that she treated the one who wanted to destroy all she loved, it was the fact that she saw through all social and territorial constraints, that she saw only a soul before her, no matter what prestige or status they may have had or not held."

Taking a moment to digest all that was being presented to her, she looked around the room in which she and George now sat. As her view flowed across the countless bookshelves her attention focused on the books contained within.

Stood side by side, each book spine held a similar glow to her own only not as bright, giving the books an appearance of being alive.

"Who do the other books belong to?" She asked George once more.

He too looked to the books sitting around them both as he spoke.

"They belong to all those you have met on your journey across the centuries," he said. "Each one containing their stories of lifetimes lived."

"Then they visit here also?" She glanced back to where they had entered the vast library.

"No, this is your building, your library."

"Then why is it filled with the stories of others as well as my own?"

"For cross reference."

Looking to the books lining the walls around her new insights came.

"Then each book here belongs to a soul I have met?"

George nodded, happy the soul beside him was becoming aware to her surroundings.

"All those you have touched or played a part of in their lives have their books here, no matter how brief or long your encounters with them were."

"It looks like I have met a lot of people then."

"Well, you have lived many lifetimes, this is shown in the size of the book before you."

Both looked to her book, each knowing of the wants inside her to read more. Taking the pages between her fingertips she turned to a new chapter ready to discover more. She stopped. Looking to the books she and George now talked of she knew that there was more to know about the lives of others presented on the bookshelves around her.

"Do some books mention me more than others?" She asked, aware George saw through her line of questioning.

"Yes, they contain your actions towards them no matter how transitory or fleeting. They tell of how you were, how you treated them in one lifetime or another."

"But, some books speak more of me than others?"

"The lifetimes of the one with the green eyes is here also," George relieved her of the needs he recognised within her.

"Am I that obvious," she felt her cheeks redden.

"Sometimes. Now, why do you think we need to see how we were with others from one lifetime to the next?"

"To see how we were with others," she repeated his words.

"But why?"

"So we can look at our actions, and," she paused. "And maybe improve how we are at times."

"Think of the security guard you would greet each morning on arriving at your work. His book is here also, written from his perspective, telling briefly how you would pay attention to his presence when all others ignored him, your actions touching his soul."

"But our connection was so brief, how can I have been important to him?"

"Maybe your time together in another lifetime was not so short lived. Maybe you were repaying the kindness he in turn had shown to you at some point during previous lives lived."

George's explanations led her to understand the reasoning behind a sometime need for cross referencing the intertwining stories of others with her own. This opened up the enormity of the complex connections her soul shared with a multitude of others.

"And each has a copy of my book in their libraries?"

"Of that they do."

"And the one with the green eyes?"

"Oh yes," George laughed. "That soul has words on you also."

Her blushes returned and she placed her fingertips back onto the pages waiting to be read on the mahogany table both she and George shared.

"Maybe there will be word of them in what you are to read now," he said before settling back in his chair once again as she began to read of another lifetime from centuries passed.

CHAPTER FIVE

The Anatolian Peninsula
Turkey
1148AD

A snap of kindling dragged him back to where he sat. Leant against humble belongings parcelled together in a makeshift hessian bag he stretched his leg out and raised its loose covering.

The camp fire's midnight glow played bright across sodden bandage. Not caring to see what lay beneath he ignored the blackening skin spreading out from meticulously applied dressing.

Sipping from the cup holding remedies prepared he added the berries harvested on his tender day's journey, knowledge learnt in his lifetime of travelling through conflicts of distant lands.

Subsiding pain caused a smile, not just for his ease but for the laughter his friends carried on settling for night.

He listened to their excitement of the approaching moments when at last they would view those Jerusalem walls dreamed of and looked to the encampment of their younger party, recalling the trepidation surrounding those trying to sleep before another day's trek and the unexpected which lay ahead of each footstep taken.

Although such times were close to thirty years in the past, he identified with a fifteen year old's mind catapulted into the wishes of an elder's religious beliefs.

Its flames far from embers, the fire cracked again as he stared to the heavens and it's a milky trail of stars, a wonder that had never left him since a boy. Only now did he consider if those pin points of light set as did the sun he had watched fall each evening, a display given in whatever country he found himself to be.

A mixture of languages swathed the darkness surrounding him. Finding seclusion in the camp fire he took in the worries of the young. All tongues seemed present.

An understanding of all languages had come to him quickly and with ease, bringing an enjoyment to the puzzle of pronouns and tenses. His daily words may have been spoken in English or French, yet his dreams would always of that he was raised, his prized Breton dialect, a salute to his Duchy under whose shield he served.

Calls from the elder camp for the young soldier's silence brought another smile to his lips on settling into the quite such demands caused.

His memories returned to Nantes, his birthplace. Remembering cobbled streets and surrounding Brittany woodlands, he wondered if the smells of freshly baked bread still flowed through the streets in dawn's awakening. A want of return hounded him and had done so since the wound which brought such discomfort had set its painful course.

Sipping once more at his concoction he thought of the others under his direction. Looking to his wound he also thought of his foolish actions.

Showing those fresh to a holy pathway how to defend themselves had resulted in his malady, a loss of footing and fall of blade seeing to a deep nick of lower limb. This incident, but weeks ago, carried a new emotion. An experience never encountered before.

Such display of defence had been performed before those captured, a failing in itself considering the dignity and secrecy his bloodlines enforced.

From the crowd of those detained one had rose to their feet, denying the advance of a foe's sword to return to their place.

Taken by the woman's persistence he had allowed her forward. What followed produced emotions hidden within him as she tended to his wound with direct approach. It had been the stares held between them when all was completed that revisited him now. An understanding of kindness entwined with the compassion of the moment, no thank you necessary, a debt repaid in a simple nod from he to her.

Moving onwards the next day after returning the homes of her kin back, he never saw her again, yet the brief exchange between them had remained since.

Looking now to his wound once more, he knew the reasons behind infection, wishing he had not taken the mud strewn path presented to him days after a stranger's healing hands.

Returning to the cosmic display above he cast away thoughts of another's selflessness and with it the pain spreading towards knee and thigh.

Apprehension regarding his wound was replaced by recollections of his younger days and his first call to arms.

Visualising himself at fifteen drew him closer to warmth than any camp fire ever could.

Watching his younger self, paintbrush in hand, he recalled those moments of joy. He also recalled his desire to add splashes of colour to the black feathers he had painted in orderly fashion across the blank white canvas of his Duchy's shields.

Those wants never came to fruition for soon his standing of artistic pursuits provided entry into Brittany's turn to rage a path across Europe and into Middle Eastern realms.

Of what was thought would take but months stretched out to years, such was the need for his skills across dented shield and torn banner, a washing of dried blood from prepared metal an often unwanted chore. That particular duty no longer remained as he reached his twentieth year. Now younger recruits where given wet rags and scrapers under the watchful eye of their master.

Toing and froing across foreign landscapes continued without a glimpse of Eastern delights promised, although one bonus came in the form of a life spent in continual sunlight as heat was at times sparse upon the streets of Nantes, its streets portraying this under a cover of what seemed perpetual shadow.

Delights of constant warmth had accompanied his years, shown now in the rugged cheek and lined brow. Raising a hand to such creases his thoughts returned to the playgrounds of youth.

His early twenties had brought with them a taste of battle, both in warfare and women. Each instance had provided their wounds. He smiled to such moments, stoking at dying flames, not only those of the camp fire keeping him company that night, but of the heated memories of another.

Jumping forwards through his years to the month following his twenty fifth birthday the Iberian Peninsula enticed concealed memories.

His service to his province under the guidance of the Church had earned him an allowance of time away from the walk of thousands.

It was of those times he remembered now on leaning back once more before amber flames.

Adept in the language, he had made for the Iberian Peninsula, intrigued by the celebrations for the coronation of Alfonso VII, and to witness the first official bullfight in honour of the new king. Since that day he had always wondered what the fight against man and bull had entailed.

Looking deep into the camp fire, now, some fifteen years later, he pushed untouched memories to the fore, a need in him to rediscover those times.

Her eyes came to him first, striking green, alive with flecks of gold. A vision of beauty held in the one who had appeared that auspicious morning on the sun drenched streets of Vera town.

Those first words said to him by the one remembered now had touched his weary soul, so used was he to fleeting encounters and the smell of battle. Although it was not the words spoken he treasured, but the slight inflection in her accent.

An understanding of language's nuances from years of travel throughout the Iberian provinces brought recognition that this young woman standing before him was not of the lands she proposed.

As is in times of a country's instability when shrouded in feud, all happened quickly, a sense of urgency urging the two to become more. With hours of their meeting he had abandoned any thought of seeing man pitted against beast in their performance of newly crowned monarchy. What was offered to him now had become all the more appealing.

And so too, he recalled his first words to her, the Turkish greeting to match the accent presented to him.

Sat alone on the Anatolian Peninsula, shrouded in memories, a smile came to him that evening towards the surprise and elation of delicate features framed by blonde curls so unlike those of her heritage.

Explanations ensued of the reasons behind her presence on foreign soil, in her distaste for the bloodshed carried out throughout Europe and the want for a new life.

Sadness entered his heart on recalling the years spent together following that day, though not for what those years contained, but for the unexpected ending which had arrived all too soon.

Revisited by a familiar pain that now cut through memories of happier times, he moved position and threw another log on the fire to fuel dwindling flames before returning to the situation which had powered his need to reach the objective location of holy war.

His twenty-eighth year had come and gone, so too had his next birthday arrived until he reached this thirtieth year. Those years spent with the one of such eyes he cherished in these moments, no more so now than he had done then. His love for another of great, kind heart and the relief of settling in one place had resulted in his turning from the life spent in the want for conquest of others in the name of prophets false and true.

Finding sanctuary on Iberia's eastern coastline they soon became part of Denya's small town community. For years the two had lived in peace, not only with themselves but in the surrounding location of their new homestead.

Thinking back on those times all these years later he realised how life had simply handed him respite from his journey, until human nature began to take its often malicious course.

Recalling that autumnal morning, surrounded by deciduous leaves showing no sign of winter's approach, he saddened to memories of laughter held before his return from gathering supplies for a planned meal on the sand bared edges of the sea each had adored. It was the heartache of never saying goodbye that had played heavy on him for all these years, plunging him back into the disillusionment of mankind he had carried before they first met.

Jealous words of others had broken his and his love's spell. A rallying of those filled with fear administrated by the bitter tongues of cassocked men.

Whisked from their home behind his back intensified the cowardice presented that day. His search for her ensued yet was never satisfied, and so he left their happiness behind beside the gentle lap of wave against Denya's shores.

His return to the fold of his youth within the ranks of his Duchy was accepted without a word. Not a question arose to his whereabouts in the previous five years, such was the respect held towards someone of experience in countless battles.

With no word to even those closest to him of his loss a new determination aroused his spirit.

Aware of the penalty for being of enemy stock, he knew his love had been taken back to her homelands. Any fears to what would confront her on her journey and final arrival were washed aside by his delving back into his chosen profession, displayed in an overwhelming want to arrive also in the fabled Jerusalem, so he may at last find his love there.

Nocturnal rustling in the surrounding woodland pulled him back into the present and his hand fell to the sword at his side. An animal's squeal loosened his grip, a welcomed intrusion to past memories.

Concern for his wound grew in being so close to the end of his journey in reuniting with the love whose memory had kept him warm on many a lonely night.

The last ten years had blurred past him, a repetitive mess of sporadic combat accompanying those blinded by religion.

The pilgrims from his own climes and further afield were always a burden to him and his company. A constant complain along treacherous paths. Although within the voyages of the weak minded he found compassion towards these misguided souls. A certain respect lay within his understanding. He identified with their unremitting want to reach the Middle Eastern city and birth right of their saviour. As he them, some peace was found in knowing of an eventual arrival to the gates of Jerusalem.

One thing had bothered him in his ten years of want in the realisation that those he had guarded had already reached their goal. They had arrived to their destination, whereas he on each occasion of nearing Jerusalem had been thrust back to the west under orders of his province, a need for his skills in craftsmanship and warfare called upon time and time again.

Knowing his abandonment of duty had been accepted once, he was sure in his knowledge that such taking of leave would not be seen so lightly again and he had submitted to commands given.

This time was different. He felt it. He was certain that by next season's fall he would walk through recaptured gates and find the one who had once given his life meaning.

Declining calls of injured wildlife matched the fading embers of the camp fire. Knowing of the journey ahead at dawn it was time now for him to retire also after an evening spent in remembrance of treasured moments spent in the arms of another.

Sitting up he winced to the pain spreading up his thigh. A reluctant look to the offending soreness gave a lightness of head causing him to settle back once more.

Wondering how the black creep of decayed flesh had spread in such haste he found solace in the stars above for the second time that night.

With thoughts of if his love now sleeping beneath the same display as he, soft words accompanied his thinking.

"You will see her again," a voice said out from the darkness.

Too weak to reach for the comfort of sword in hand, he instead found security in that the words spoken to him now were in his beloved Breton dialect.

"You have taken a journey of such undertaking," the voice came again.

He looked to its source, his sight finding the figure now stood beside him.

"Now it is time to rest," the man reached out his hand.

Taking the stranger's gentle clasp, he watched the fire's orange glow overcome by a whiteness so pure of which he had never encountered before. Relaxing back, his eyes closed, his breathing slowing under new found ease.

Any disappointment in not reaching Jerusalem's walls eased also, replaced by the promise of looking into those green eyes once more and the flecks of gold dancing within them.

CHAPTER SIX

A film of tears accompanied her gaze on leaving the book and staring out through the windows above.

Soon becoming lost in the falling darkness outside she looked to the first stars that approached the night, a subtle appearance inviting every observer to watch their display.

As had the one who had trekked in vain through freezing temperatures in search of a new home for his family, and the one read of now on his route towards Jerusalem, in her days as a teenager she too had always been captivated by the milky stream of stars that would visit the night skies each evening, bringing an added joy to accompany the rhythmic swish of the ocean's call against ever moving sands.

Longing for that line of stars to arrive now her wishes would not be reached for a few more hours and she wondered where the book would take her in that time before seeing her comforting cosmic sight.

Leaving the view of outside a single tear fell from her.

"You had a difficult journey," George said.

"I did." she bowed her head, wiping her cheeks as sorrow rose within her heart to what had passed. "Those green eyes were never seen again."

"Not in that lifetime at least."

"Or in my last."

"But they have been encountered many times before and so shall they again." George could see his words gave little consolation. "And who do you think those eyes belong to?"

Gazing back up to the night sky, once again she yearned for its display to come forth, to dissect the darkness and so maybe numb the heartache surrounding her now.

George recognised her needs. Reaching for her hand as he had always done he waited for her eyes to meet with his.

"Feel no sorrow," he said on her return to him. "For you have shared many lifetimes together, and as I have spoken of before, so shall you again."

Thoughts of being reunited with the soul they talked of now reduced her heartache.

"I feel so silly," she laughed through her tears. "I mean, the only knowledge I have of the one with green eyes is either in the chapters I read with you or the brief moments we spent together in my last lifetime. I don't understand how the loss of someone I have such little memory of can affect me so."

"Who do you think those green eyes belong to?"

Wiping her face free of tears she knew her answer within moments.

"My soul mate," she said. "But how can I know this? How do I know who this soul is each time we meet?"

"Because you are what the description says, soul mates. Two souls destined to be together in each lifetime should you meet or not."

"Should we meet?"

"Yes, for even if your paths are not to cross during one lifetime, there will always be that awareness that they are somewhere out there. A pulling on your own soul that another's soul aches for your presence also."

"So, if we're not to meet then it's ok knowing they are out there somewhere in the world?"

"Yes, but why do you think you don't meet each and every lifetime?"

"That I don't know," she said.

George sensed a slight ire in her words, the tempestuous nature he had watched play out for centuries rearing its head again.

"Sometimes we must spend a lifetime alone," he told her.

"But why?"

"There are many reasons, so a soul may learn individuality, learning to be comfortable alone and not gain their own identity from that of being with another. Only through such a process of aloneness can a soul be next to the one they are destined to be with. Only then can they truly be with another who knows them as well as they do they."

Taking stock of his words to her, she looked to the surrounding bookcases and shelves wondering where the book belonging to the soul they talked of now was kept.

"I can show you where to find if you would like," George understood what she searched for now.

"No," she whispered on turning to him. "I must read more of my own lifetimes before that of another's."

George nodded to her, delighted by her understanding of matters of the heart.

"You know we have many soul mates?" He said.

"There are more than one?"

"Yes, the one we speak of now concerns love in the form of romantic ventures. Do you not think there are possibly other kinds of soul mates met with on our paths through time?"

Shrugging to his questioning, George continued his chain of thought.

"We have bonds with all the souls we meet with. This produces soul mates of differing titles. Have you never met someone who you feel so alive with when all you ever do is simply have coffee together? Has there not been a soul you had met in the street by chance and got on so well with it felt as if you had always known them?"

"These are soul mates too?"

"Under different headings, yes, of course they are. Your links are present, growing stronger with each lifetime coming and going. Your coffee soul mate, your opportune stranger soul mate. There are even souls you may meet with and argue."

"Arguing soul mates?"

"Believe it or not, yes. But the moments you spend arguing with these souls eventually fades and often results in a friendship that deepens through the lifetimes to come. For you cannot argue and fight forever."

"So really, everyone can be classed as a soul mate?"

"This is true, but think of it another way. Can you see how we are all linked, each soul we meet, laugh, cry and sometimes argue with? In recognising the connection we have with each soul, this in turn leads us to seeing how any animosity or hostility felt for another is futile. For where is the sense in battling with a soul that has such close associations with our own."

As George's words began to course through her understanding of others, she leant back in her chair and looked through the tall windows before the table they sat at.

George also looked up to the stars establishing their place across the night sky, a relentless development that would soon display the wanted formation so often met with by the soul beside him.

Together they stared upwards, lost in the comfort of one another, much the way they had always. This she acknowledged now, her understanding to such matters growing with every word read or spoken by this man with kind eyes who showed her so much. Taking her view from the display above she looked to the one who continued to stare to the stars, her memories of his features beginning to appear.

"You meet with me every time?" She asked him.

"Of that I do," he replied, his view not leaving the night skies.

"Do I recognise you each time?"

"In a way."

"Then why am I struggling to remember you now?"

George looked to her.

"Because sometimes it is better to forget all that has gone before."

His words only confused her more. Wondering in what way it was better to forget as George had put it, her full attention fell to him in search for an answer.

"The stories of your previous lives you have read here beside me have already filled your heart with expectation and longing," George began to explain. "Can you see how if you knew all that had happened, if all you had experienced in life were to be recalled with ease, there would be no freshness to your world, no excitement towards the new moments met with on each of your subsequent lifetimes."

"But I remember some things," she said, memories of those green eyes burning bright within her.

"Sometimes glimpses of lifetimes past come to each and every soul. Remnants of intense emotions carried through from across the centuries."

"And I always know who you are when you appear in my final moments?"

"Yes, and with my presence comes an understanding that it is time to leave all you think you have ever known, your hand in mine on each occasion."

Casting her view upwards to the stars once more, she began to understand George's words on the amnesia felt within her now.

George felt her awareness evolve beside him. His want to aid her understanding balanced by his consideration concerning the discovery of self-awareness.

"Look at it this way," he said. "Would the chapters you read now hold any fascination for you if you knew their stories already, if you knew all of what was to happen to those you read of?"

A smile came to her, George's words giving her peace of mind that was coupled by a want to continue reading the book sat on the table before them.

"I saw the shield," she said, "all those feathers…" her words faded as recollections of her painting those same feathers she had looked to in the gallery's basement rooms came to her. Memories of sitting on the roadside of North Africa nearly one thousand years ago entered her heart. As distinct and vivid as could be, these recollections sealed her understanding that the ones she read of were in fact her, that she was the same soul who had lived many times before.

"Now you see how you are linked," George said to her.

"It was me," she said, her eyes wide. "And so was the old doctor," she added, her mind filling with memories of her journey three hundred years earlier than the life of a French knight, and along an English beachfront that would mark the last moments of a lifetime spent once more in the service of others.

"As are all the lives you are to read of," George motioned to the book waiting for her attention. "Every lifetime contained within these pages holds the actions and choices you have made. Each chapter a telling of who you were, what you believed in," he leant closer to her. "The true essence your soul has carried throughout time."

Placing her hand back onto the book she felt its warmth. Comfort came to her once more.

Any trepidation she may have experienced at one time in delving into lifetimes lived dissolved as the safety she now basked in at George's side overtook all other emotions.

Leaning forwards she reached for the book again and with a smile turned its pages to the start of a new chapter.

CHAPTER SEVEN

Basilica di Santa Croce
The Republic of Florence, Italy
1322AD

Scratches of pen on paper echoed throughout the chamber, the shuffle of parchment accompanying the marks of scribes.

Concentration reigned high amongst the fifteen men, even though the noise of construction played out in intermittent bursts of melodic thuds and crashes.

With building underway of twelve extra chapels and several annexes, the literary order of Franciscans had been cast to the rear of holy ground, bringing dissatisfaction to most, none more so than one whose dreams out matched those of his compatriots.

A keen eye on his work, leant over his board, he neared completion of his sanctified illustration. To some it may have been simply an introduction to their saviour's words, a small box in the upper left hand corner of the page, filled with bright shades of capital letter initiating a start of parable, but to him it meant release to his soul.

He had tried to convince the head friar to allow him to solely focus on these designs. Telling of his wants and how the calligraphy of those aged words that followed held no joy he was soon reprimanded. He recalled now the wrath presented to him in his request, how the meaning of austerity was drilled into him by a Greyfriar well past his prime. Walking from that confrontation he had wondered of his received lecture on the stain of original sin. Had it been so wrong to consume from that mythical tree of knowledge, was a heart's want to learn more truly the fall of man as depicted?

Looking to his small masterpiece he summoned the patience now needed to fill the remainder of the page with neatly placed black lettering. A duty needed to be performed before the next illustration would present itself to him. Wading through those words of Latin tongue his heart wandered to the approaching lunch hour and how he would achieve his confirmations of beauty in art.

Each day he would concoct a plan allowing him entrance to Santa Croce's newest chapel. It was there that he would stand unnoticed, his view centred on the skilled brushstrokes of a master artist, his biblical scenes mapped out in gigantic fresco for all to see in shades of blues and whites. How his soul yearned to paint on such a large scale, saddened his skills were confined to mere corners of dried paper.

He pulled the heavy brown robes to him, the ones that had kept him warm since first taken in by kindly monks who had found him on Florentine streets begging and of no home. Now, in this, his twenty-ninth year, he recalled a five year old's stare to the food presented to him that first night beneath rooftops of belief and charity.

Tempted to pull his cowl over bared scalp he resisted. Thinking of the repercussions his argument of coldness would produce his spirit calmed. Wrapping his robe closer to him he wondered why he and his brothers had been put in the rear of holy grounds and place of no sun. Was it not they who now transcribed the word of God?

Cold bit into his fingertips. Still he wrote on. Every letter finished a step closer to the drawing of religious tales.

Looking to those sat around him, he saw his antics had raised a smile within them. They knew of his abhorrence to the cold, and of his fire towards the injustice often experienced from their elders. A wanton desire to break their tedium evolved from the feisty outbursts they had watched their brother execute so often.

These stares he felt now pushed his wants for more than the repetitious strokes of ink he made each day. Another pull on his robing caused a giggle from the back of the room prompting the arrival of stern glares from the old monk sat before them.

Knowing those eyes of authority would fall to him first an air of defiance came in reply. This he would admit was much exaggerated so to produce the stifled laughter now flowing around him. His desired outcome caused the head friar to stand.

A dressing down was fuelled by a casting of ink tipped pen across the room, its thrower sent to his quarters, proud of the glee given to his brothers that morning.

A smile accompanied the walk to his room. Now he too could join the emotions and tribulations of others in the outside world, albeit in the prose concealed within the confines of his bunk.

Hurried footsteps explained his want to read more of the manuscript smuggled onto hallowed ground.

Although its words were not looked upon as heresy, it was nonetheless concealed from the eyes of those of little faith or those who it seemed walked a different path than stated under the instruction of the Papal States.

Walking into his room and closing the door shut behind him away from prying eyes, the young monk considered the banishment of the words awaiting his arrival hidden beneath his mattress. Reaching for the leather bound manuscript he lay back on his bed and opened its pages, thinking why it was banned from those of their own mind.

He had seen his treasured poem's author may times upon the Florentine streets. Only now after reading his words did he regret not talking to him. These wishes had been taken from him with the death of the poet whose works now lay in his hands only one year passed.

Of the six months the author's visions had been in his possession, he was now on his third reread. On his first he had devoured each word, becoming adept in days with the vernacular Italian in which it was written, so different to the clinical Latin of which he was used to. Enjoyment also came in the illustrations presented to him, more so in the knowledge that his artistry reached a similar proficiency of deftness.

A little guilt would visit him from time to time, wondering if the elderly friar who led his company of scribes and the one who berated him often knew it was he who had borrowed the manuscript of concealed words from him.

As was usual, his guilt faded as soon as it appeared and he leant back, manuscript propped up on his knees. Finding his place of times in purgatory, he thought back to the first part of the epic poem's trilogy.

Studies of the underworld's eternal inferno had not brought any fear to him, for as its main character had done so also, he felt safe at the Roman poet's side who guided them both through relentless pyres.

Finding parallels within his own studies he became absorbed by the tales of netherworlds unseen. One such story intrigued him most. Never before had he ever considered the fortune tellers and soothsayers of this world. Although finding comfort in his bunk he had shuddered to the penalty for such acts, the spending of an eternity walking around with head on backwards, the penance for trying to see a future not yet experienced whilst in mortal life.

Lessons learnt under Santa Croce's instruction were present also in the text read now.

Fascinated by the stories of those living in purgatory he delved deeper into the theology behind these seven deadly sins which both repulsed and excited him.

Tales of love amid the nine rings of Mount Purgatory brought new insights to one who had always lived amongst men, astounded by the complexity such an emotion carried.

Explanations of the excessive love held in the sins of Lust, Greed and Gluttony almost counteracted that of deficient feeling of the heart represented by Sloth, when love given was not depicted as being strong enough. It would be the third collection of the sins of Wrath, Envy and Pride that shocked him most, for he had no inclination that there could be such a thing as malicious love.

Assured that these sins would meet with their antidotes of the seven heavenly virtues found within the manuscript's final part of Paradise, he anticipated the arrival of Chastity, Temperance, Charity, Diligence, Patience, Kindness and Humility to appear from the epic poem's baring of the soul and all contained within.

Continuing to read that day alone in his room with not a care towards banishment from his board, he could not have imagined the life he was to lead, prompted by the words of a fellow resident of Florence.

A want to experience the world had ignited inside him, his epiphany coming in recognising the poet's overriding message to his readers of the divine, to not only find God, but to harbour the desire to find oneself.

Forli
The Papal States
1324AD

Bathed in afternoon sunlight he took delight in the searing heat across cheek and brow before opening his eyes.

Looking to the buildings and people of the Forli city-commune as they played out their day, the scene showed no evidence of the long trial as depicted in the portrayal of Inferno's never ending penances.

Having just arrived to the city walls read of yet never seen he took to the Forli streets with vigour, eager to witness all around him, on this, his first true stop on his quest to discover not only himself but the human condition that captivated him so.

Lanes and alleyways lined his path. As his footsteps fell between shadow and rich sunbeam he recalled the moments that had caused his arrival to this point just days before.

His treasured book's words had lain heavy upon him. Not so much as the atonements given to those of easy virtue, but in a pulling on his soul, a pushing for him to seek the experiences of life described.

It was not until the eve of his thirty-first birthday that the ache of a want for a new life overwhelmed his heart.

As with a flower bud must leave its enclosed shell of safety, his desire to bloom came too much and so resulted in releasing hidden tensions from within.

The speed of his departure from a monastic life known for so long came of little surprise to those who truly knew him.

Standing that morning outside Santa Croce's marbled finery, preparing to take his first steps into the unknown, a familiar face had approached him.

Not a word came from the elderly friar who had observed the yearning of a young man's want to explore grow. The one he knew held such great potential. For years he had watched his artistry develop alongside feisty temperament, and although the outbursts directed at him were often a distraction to his faith, the old master of scribes had secretly enjoyed those moments of youth's verve and fire.

Pausing for a moment on those Forli streets he remembered the moment aged hands had presented the manuscript he had returned to his master's desk the evening before.

A simple nod was all that passed between the two on the receiving of such a gift, somehow each knowing it would be needed on his intended journey of discovery.

Continuing onwards through Forli's community he sensed the manuscript kept safe within his humble belongings cast in a small bag across sunburnt shoulder, packed tight between the changes of clothes similar to the ones he now wore. How strange it felt to be in civilian attire now.

The robes that had encased him for most of his life were gone. Only the tonsure of shaved scalp betrayed his new appearance, yet he knew the sign of a life lived in religious study would soon grow out in the passing of time.

Leaving Forli's walls that day he thought of what was to come on his arrival to the coastal city of Ravenna. A wondering of where to visit first on his journey evolved from the respect given to his inspiration's text. It seemed only fitting that he should be where the author of the poem he held so dear had taken his last breathes upon this world.

Walking eastwards towards the calling of Adriatic seas, his thoughts returned to what would greet him on his arrival once arriving at the Papal State's northern most city.

Memories of the penalty given to the fortune tellers came to him and he shunned his want to know of uncertain futures, continuing onwards, with a heart filled with the newfound delights of freedom.

Within days of leaving Forli, his destination loomed. Deciding on approaching the city from its famous coastline a walk towards Ravenna's eastern ramparts provided a view of entry into city walls.

On his trek beneath late afternoon sun in the remnants of summer months, he knew not of what was to greet him. A sight which would stay with him always.

Tired from his walk he pushed onwards over shale and rock, the fine grains of sand mingled within his chosen path indicating a closing arrival.

Watching the sun begin a steady decent and it accompanying fall into orange shades he reached the brow of his last climb and looked before him in wonder.

In all is years he had never seen such sights. His years within the confines of Florence's city territories had not permitted him to see the waters he knew flanked his republic's western shores. Still he had yet to see the splendour the Ligurian Sea gave, but his first view of blue salt waters was that of the Adriatic and in his eyes this was enough.

In the advent of dusk he made his way to the shoreline, taking off his boots to find comfort for aching feet in the shallow depths where parched sands met with surf.

Standing in his new experience of wave lapping against shin and knee his want of adventure and discovery were confirmed in those moments, with any doubts toward leaving Santa Croce's security lost to him then and there and for the rest of his days.

The week that followed saw his visit to the poet's final moments and he kept his promise made to himself of observing all around him. By the end of that week he had found work in a small bakery along the seafront, a small room provided also above the premises in which to bunk.

Early starts needed for dough's rise were of no concern to him as this allowed time for his two pleasures of the evening.

Each evening he would sit alone before dusk at the same spot he had first discovered his love for the sea, watching the sun delve into a far horizon of glowing pinks and reds. This was always followed by his second pleasure of night time's hours, the intimate study of his prized manuscript.

It would be a whole month before restlessness of spirit entered his heart. For although he had found a place of peace, work he enjoyed and a seascape of constant beauty, a want to push further into the unknown pervaded him. Within days he had accepted to what his soul craved and left the shores of Ravenna behind him.

Moving northwards he left the Papal States and entered in to the territory of the Republic of Venice. Making its main city a temporary home he found work once more with little effort in one of many glassware factories and a new home beside a myriad of rippling canal and waterway.

The weeks passed and he enjoyed his work and although he missed the sea, solace was found in the slow flowing waters surrounding his daily life.

So too did he enjoy his time amongst the Venetians, much as he had done so with Ravenna's people of easy manner and smiles.

For two months his life became his own, one filled with daytime routines of work and evenings of play. Such was his energy for life during those times his only sadness came as an inherent disquiet entered his thoughts once more. The want to explore more resulted in a leaving of the place considered a joy to be within.

Leaving northwards for the new climbs of Verona, he questioned this incessant want of moving onwards that pulled on his soul. In the knowledge that he would one day find his answers, he submitted to the calls of his heart, travelling in peace of mind that everything was playing out as it was supposed to be.

His visit to Verona would prove brief. With only an afternoon spent in the city before heading west to Milan, he afforded himself a meal in Verona's main square. Although his lunch of cheese, bread and slices of succulent tomato was that of simple tastes he enjoyed his extravagance, a reward he considered for the journey he now took, his voyage of discovery in all around him.

Milan too would be a momentary stopover. Once more he gained pleasure formed in the taking of lunch amid grand piazzas of ornate beauty. The simplicity of his needs and joys of the ordinary gave him the understanding that he was experiencing all he had desired when dressed in robes at his scribe's board.

These insights furthered his questions of constant movement from city to city, village to town. Thoughts towards why his travels were so transitory came to him that afternoon, his stomach full and heart light. Was it that there was a destination to which he was meant to arrive, and if so it seemed, in haste?

Travelling by day and finding rest on the northern plains of the Duchy of Savoy's territories, he continued his reading of the friars parting gift to him.

Each turn of page offered him new insights into the world around him and enhanced an optimism towards unknown futures he knew he would arrive at when he was supposed to and not a moment sooner, or he now realised, later.

With lightness of step and being, he enjoyed his walk through Turin streets, yet he felt this was not to be his home and so moved southwards, away from the slight chill he had become unaccustomed too.

Genoa would prove a different welcome on his soul, of which he would always remember, for within its walls he was greeted with such kindness and generosity he felt for sure that this was the place he was meant to arrive at on his journey.

Weary from the short visits to cities of no consequence to him, the greetings found on arrival made him determined to once more find work and a place to call his own. These wants came forth on one of many fishing vessels that sailed the Ligurian waters he had dreamed of. So too did he find a home, a small room maybe, but it held two specific treasures, one a window with a view onto the sea that could be taken whilst laying on his bed, the other coming in the form of another window, this time positioned above his pillow. Now he could enjoy the milky stream of stars in comfort that had kept him amazed and in good company when sleeping on the roadsides of his travels.

A month soon passed, and then another with no sign of meeting the restlessness that frequently crept up in the guise of unwanted visitor.

Enjoying his mornings at sea and the eventual arrival back to port in the mid-afternoon with the day's catch, he continued his good living and the new found camaraderie with is crew. This enjoyment of life would continue for six whole months until one summer's morning aboard his workplace of stern and sail, when the cravings of uninvited caller upon his soul returned.

In knowledge of the signs unrest carried, amid the now searing heat reflected off waves of green salt ridden waters, a similar sadness came as had been experienced on the shores of Ravenna.

Embracing his push to move forwards to whatever awaited his arrival he kept his thoughts of departure to himself, enjoying the last moments with those he knew he must leave also.

On their arrival to port that afternoon with a boat laden with more fish than ever before, the rich bonus each fisherman received for such a haul confirmed his decisions to find pastures new. The extra weight of coin in his pocket told that now was the time and within days he was gone.

Finding temporary work aboard one of the boats that ferried passengers southwards alongside the western stretches of Ligurian waters, he wondered in passing if Naples was a place he would call home.

On is eventual arrival to the vast port he made his way across Naples' bustling harbour. Stopping to the smells of freshly baked bread he walked to stalls filled with fruits and vegetables from lands bordering the Mediterranean Sea.

Simple tastes came to him again in the sight of an apple stall squeezed between other vendors. Attracted to its shining display thoughts towards what his arrival to Naples would ensue accompanied his approach.

Choosing an apple that would prove to be his lunch, his answers to unknown futures came in the unexpected sight of the stall holder's delicate beauty framed by curls of blonde hair. He knew then that he had reached his destination as he became lost in eyes of green and gold.

Naples
The Kingdom of Naples
1380AD

The calls of grandchildren echoed throughout the house and onto the porch facing the calm waters of the Gulf of Naples.

Sat watching the waves roll back and forth before him, he smiled to the laughter resounding through is home. Recalling his youth, his memories filled with a similar jollity found within the confines of Santa Croce.

Many years had passed since those days. Now in his eighty-seventh year he could still recall all that had happened in those times.

Peering out onto silver surf, tinges of green waters caught in sunlight brought with them memories of another. It had been a month since her passing, yet still he could feel her presence, as much as he had the day he had bought that apple from her on the harbour front of the city he had come to call home.

Holding his cherished leather bound manuscript in his lap he gave a moment to thank the old friar who had given these words to him. He was thankful to him for the experiences he had been shown, yet no more so for providing direction towards the one found at the end of his journey.

Finding peace in recalling the eyes he had looked into for over fifty years he heard a shuffle of feet behind him.

"Yes," a voice said to him. "It is time now."

Reassured by the words of the man stood beside him now, he smiled out to the seas he had always valued. Memories came to him of the life begun on the streets of Florence before progressing to the sanctuary of prayer and then onwards in discovery of what the world had to offer.

"You have had quite the journey," the voice knew of his thoughts.

A nod came in reply, as did the receiving of the man's hand in his as both became wrapped in light, its pureness cast across the leather covers of prized manuscript.

CHAPTER EIGHT

Her fingers lingered on the last page of the chapter. George knew of her thoughts, of the contentment wrapped around her, soothing her emotions towards the one she craved to know more of.

"He found her," she said. "They spent a lifetime together."

"Of that they did," George confirmed her words, adding to her awareness that it was in fact she who had begun life as a monk and had eventually become a family man for the majority of her years.

George watched her understanding fall into place, allowing him to press forwards with his questioning.

"But first let us talk of how you can identify with the one you have just read of. What similarities can you see run true within you today?"

Recollections of biblical scenes came to her, a mixture of memories swarming as she saw herself not only painting the opening illustrations of parable and psalm, but also restoring the very same etchings several hundred years later.

"And of his desire to travel, his desire to see the world and all it had to offer," George asked. "Do you feel a link with such wants?"

"I never really travelled," she replied, trying to find the connection between needs of a fourteenth century monk and herself.

"But you followed very similar paths."

"In what way?"

"You both left you childhood home did you not?"

"Yes, I suppose we did."

"And who did you find in doing so?"

With thoughts leading back to those brief moments shared in the doorway of a midtown New York coffee shop the connections George gently coaxed from her came to light.

"The monk found the one with green eyes, the same way I did far away from the life I had always led."

"Yes, although those moments had been brief for you, many lifetimes ago years were spent with the one destined to be with."

"The pull you talked of earlier, was it my heart leading me to leave my home and travel across the country for a new life, so I could meet with the one I have always known?"

"You partook on a journey."

"Like I did when I was a monk? And a knight too come to think of it."

"There are many types of journeys. But there is one overriding factor that must be observed for said travels to be a success."

"To follow your heart," she said, the tenacious spirit glimpsed within her previous lifetimes appearing once more. "There is no other way," she added, her calm expression portraying the utmost certainty of her beliefs.

Recognising the feisty yet confident spirit he had always stood next to, George waited for her to elaborate on her statement.

"It's the most important thing," she continued.

"Of that it is, and why?"

"Because it leads you to where you should be."

George's pleasure in seeing her awareness play out before him became evident in his smiles.

"Sometimes," he said, "the paths we at time take are not of our own liking. Often a soul walks towards what is expected of them, a direction that has been designated and plotted out for them for the rest of their days. But you know as I what is needed to stray away from expectation."

Taking his lead she too began to smile, her realisations confirmed by reading of the past lives once held.

"It takes courage," she said.

"Great courage indeed, a bravery that is in every soul but is often never explored."

"Explored?"

"Each and every soul may have an equal amount of bravery dwelling within them, yet it is not each soul that acts upon such desires of searching for..."

"For their soul mate?" She interrupted.

"No, not necessarily. Can you think of another soul that you may want to discover and befriend?"

Looking around to the numerous books lining the library walls she considered taking a book at random from its place and searching for her answer.

"The answers are within you," George knew of her wishes. "Follow your own heart towards what you seek, you will find your solution there."

Taking his advice and settling back in her seat she closed her eyes. In moments she found herself in the meditative world in which she had found such peace in her last lifetime. New ideas came to her. On opening her eyes her thoughts filled with questions, prompted by her questioning of where her ability to meditate came from.

"Maybe we shall find that out as we continue reading your book," George said, aware as ever of her thoughts. "But for now, have you reached your answer towards who a soul at times yearns to discover?"

"I have," she laughed. "It was so obvious,"

"It is, but not all understand the notion, let alone take the journey towards finding who we talk of now."

Both fell silent and looked once again to the windows set high above them. Lost in the growing array of stars and galaxies they relaxed into their respite from talk of affairs of the heart. Each knew they had an eternity to read through her book and those that sat around them if needed. Time had no place here, an unspoken fact which she somehow already knew. Only her burgeoning curiosity kept the pace, her inquisitive nature longing to know all. With this in mind she turned to George.

"It is me I wanted to discover," she told him. "It was me who I took a journey towards, so I may understand how I am. How I perceive myself."

"The exploration of self is the greatest journey a soul can take. It matters not if such a path covers immense distances or not. For the search is internal."

"Then why did the monk, did I, go out into the world? Could I not have found myself on the holy grounds where I was raised?"

"Sometimes this is the way, but remember, the young monk identified that the life he was living as a scribe was not his true path. This is often the first step towards self-realisation."

"To understand that you are not on your right path?"

"Yes, only then can a soul begin to make steps towards finding its true vocation, fuelled also by the unconscious pulling towards their forthcoming soul mate."

"Then what other steps are needed? How many steps are there?"

"Questions, questions," George laughed. "It all depends on the individual soul, and of course, how far they are willing to go towards finding that of which they seek."

These words entered her conscious more than any others that had been shared between them and she began to see the courage they talked of, the daring needed within a soul to take the winding path ways towards self-discovery.

"Time alone," she said, her voice a whisper as the enormity of such a journey flourished within her own soul.

"Solitude is needed in the early stages of the search for understanding," George said. "This is the first hurdle that a soul often falls at when attempting its journey."

"Through fear of being alone," she knew also of such things, her memories serving her well of her first few months living in the anonymity all great metropolises hold.

"Aloneness allows us to explore the facets of our character which often remain hidden when in the company of others, be they close family, friends or strangers."

"Allowing us to grow," her voice remained soft, her realisations triggering recollections of the lives read of.

Staring into the night sky she remembered the loneliness experienced on the snow laden landscapes over twenty thousand years passed and how those times had helped her find the fighting spirit buried deep within her soul, a trait that would be identified in both the old doctor of medieval England and within the nature of Brittany's wounded knight.

Focusing on the story just read a different aspect had been brought forward by the monk's experiences of solitude. Gentleness of spirit had been allowed to emerge, coupled by the good humour this soul held, bringing life around him an added shine often lost by those whose innocence has at one time been cast aside, set adrift in view of being an emotion of little use in the dealing with others and life itself.

Once again George read her thoughts. Of this she knew and felt comfort in his understanding of her ideas and notions. An understanding reached between them that had been present for eons.

"And of the monk," he said to her, "was he always alone?"

Recalling the final pages of the monk's lifetime, she smiled to her own memories of seeing those green eyes that played such an integral part to her soul's story.

"No," she said. "He made..." her words trailed away as renewed awareness flooded her senses.

"He made what?" George pressed.

"He made a choice."

"What kind of choice?"

"The choice to abandon his search and to spend a lifetime with the one he loved."

"This is true, but can you see that he did not abandon his search."

She stared at George, her mind trying to find an answer once again. That answer soon came to her, producing a broad smile on its conception.

"His search continued within the undertaking of sharing his life with another soul."

"And so he explored another facet of itself," George accompanied her contentment in discovering not only a new characteristic within those she spoke of now, but more so a fresh identification of her own being, her own soul. "Like a diamond," George said in recognition of her discoveries. "So many faces, so many facets, each one waiting to be found, to be polished, looked upon and admired."

Looking to the book eagerness shone in her eyes within his description of the soul., her need to read and discover overtaking all other thoughts.

George recognised her drive, something he had seen in her from the first when reaching for the cold fingers of a man who had tried his best to cross a freezing wilderness in search of better pastures. So too had he witnessed such keenness surrounding the old doctor who had ignored the word of her master in order to follow her own path.

Looking to the young woman beside him already turning a page to the story telling of her next lifetime he saw each quality shine within her.

Saying nothing he watched her begin to read, aware of the next characteristic that would come to display itself.

CHAPTER NINE

Madrid, Spain
1478AD

She tried not to slip, to keep balance on the wet stone lane they both rushed through now. Constant rains had accompanied their path from dawn and into their arrival at city walls on a journey to find salvation promised.

Lifting a rain soaked cowl from her, she looked to her husband. In seeing the worry in his eyes had intensified since stepping onto Madrid's dangerous grounds she reached out to him, placing a gentle hand on his that was not rebuked.

Reassured by her touch he summoned a smile before nodding in the direction of their next street to race through.

The mid December weather had hindered their progress, coldness of nights proving a burden after a day filled with the exertion of much needed secrecy. They had not considered this in the one week of planning held on hearing news of November's newly found grounds for unfair trial.

An escape to the northern reaches of Alpine retreat had been considered, but word of supposed battles between Swiss and Milanese forces for control of valuable mountain passes had put paid to that option, that and the thought of even colder temperatures of which both deplored.

Their continued race through alleyway and lanes amid those unaware of their plight captured a poise of steadiness and stealth, a combination much needed as not to alert the suspicions of others around them.

She looked to her love once more, his glance back to her giving all she needed. This time it was she who was reassured. That comfort came in a wink filled with the knowing of their destination and that they were together in their quest for safe passage to foreign lands.

Fuelled by such declarations held in silence she marched onwards at his side, aware of the steely Castilian blood that coursed strong through his veins, as did it hers also.

Travelling from their home of Segovia, their journey signalled by leaving the mighty doorway of San Andres, they had looked back to the city walls of their birth in the day's unfolding of twilight, each hesitant towards unknown futures yet to arrive.

Walking through the night south-eastwards towards Madrid's call, they had used the milky stream of stars above as reference for a fast arrival to their destination. Only those flickering pinpoints of light knew of their departure. Talk of the disappearance of the young couple who had helped so many would be rife amongst those on Segovia's streets and within marble floored plaza. Of this she knew, hopeful their plan to be in the place they would be considered to have most avoided to be of wise choice.

From her husband's slight increase of pace she knew they were nearing their goal. His talk of the man they must meet with had occupied the conversations between them.

Sure that he had been in great demand since November's official forming of inquisition, the want of finding the one who assured escape from the hands of interrogators gave them reason to continue through building rain and the onset of hunger's cry.

It had seemed odd to her their meeting should not take place on the coastlines of which they could sail from safely, but in the very areas under the tight scrutiny of the Suprema, the headquarters of the Grand Inquisitor and Council of the Supreme Inquisition. Releasing doubts held she had in turn put her trust into the love for her husband, as had he given his faith to the one who now assured them with talk of escape.

Neither could understand the looming threat now concerning them both. This questioning hounded their thoughts.

So many had come to them from within Segovia's walls as had those from afar, presenting their malaise to the couple who were known throughout Spain's northern grasps for their adeptness in matters of healing others.

Here now, just a few weeks following the legal foundations of inquisition, they had fled their homelands in knowledge of what may come. They could not believe that the act of helping others with the aid of local berries and plant life was now construed as heresy, not only in the eyes of the Church but in those of the ones who now ruled.

An inevitable confrontation with these oppressors would soon arise, of this both knew, yet it seemed impossible for them to be intended victims of new rules, when Isabella I of Castile herself had sent one of her many courtesans to them to provide a concoction for an ailment of much privacy and wanted secrecy from her king.

As was the case of small communities, word had soon spread of their treatment of royals, leading to the popularity towards their skills in the healing of others. How this word was spread both did not know having kept the discretions of noble birth close to them.

The rain gave some let up on the last of the maze of stony lane between flanking homes. Knowing the respite those tall walls gave in the city's summer months, she longed for the hot rays that would dry the clothing laying heavy across her shoulders now.

Adjusting the cowl disguising defined cheekbones gained in a heritage of Basque ancestry, the affliction of hooded cloak would be of great help she knew within the male dominated tavern they would soon have cause to enter.

That place of men at one time would have frightened her. This had been in her younger days. Here in flight from the repressors of Spain's intellect and progress fire burnt within her heart, provoking a same feistiness she would sometimes administer in portions when needs were justified.

As the tavern appeared before them her husband laughed on looking to her, not only on their finding of location, but of the vigour he recognised in her.

A want to hold hands came though was avoided and with bodies close but not touching they drew nearer to their goal until pushing on large oak doors and entering into the realm of the undesirable yet needed.

The tavern was misleading from its outside portrayal. Its new visitors looked into cavernous dim light of tucked away corners and shaded booths spread outward from either side of a long bar of customers. The greatest source of light, they made for the bar, a place of safety for them both amongst adverse clientele.

It pained him to leave her. She nodded to him, assurance in her stare of fire of which not even he would have dared to cross.

Pulling her cowl across her features she watched him go then looked to the solitary barmaid, a comfort found in this masculine territory.

Her thoughts retuned to the home they had left. Considering if she would ever walk its rooms and gardens again, her heart led her to the plants and fruits that had provided cures for so many. Memories of the artistic flair shown in designing her plot brought new questions of if she would have a similar garden in the lands both were promised now, and of the safety held within.

Giving up all they had on the words of another aroused suspicion to swim inside her. A want of confirmation nagged on her soul. She knew her instincts would come forward on meeting with the man her husband now searched for. The knowing of things she harboured within had been called upon many times before, only this time she understood the full baring her correct assumptions would imply.

A hand on her shoulder signalled her love's return. Safe at one another's side again she prepared her intuition to guide their path.

Those standing at the bar watched them walk away, as did the barmaid who then peered over to the tavern's far walls. Her concern for the young woman of beauty and her partner with such striking eyes remained hidden from her expression, she too knowing her actions were under scrutiny also.

Unaware of the stares held upon them both, the young couple of Segovia entered a private both leaving all looks behind them.

A lone candle in the centre of the table between them cast an amber glow across the three.

Trying to discern the man's features proved difficult in such low light conditions as he spoke. She glanced to her husband in his introduction to her. Keeping quiet and so adding to her false representations of demur she smiled to the man across the table from her, trying once again to surmise if he was to be friend or foe.

Knowing the reasons behind her submissive manner her husband was more than aware of the cunning and intellect his wife would now call upon. Taking the lead he began to negotiate with the man they had come to meet.

Portly cheeks were the first sign of distaste she held towards their so called saviour. Such an appearance in these times of austerity showed through in this way, where those of little retained a slim stature. Greed came to her thoughts.

Intermittent laughter would come from the man, his apparent lack of seriousness towards their case giving rise to her instincts of distrust towards he who had given his word of reliance.

A want to leave grew in her mind and she placed a hand on her husband's knee aware his thoughts mirrored hers.

Without a word she waited for their cue. None came and the man continued his diatribe of mutterings with no mention of the safety he had told her husband he could provide.

Anxiety raised its head as feeling of distrust escalated in her abhorrence for this man's betrayal of given word. She felt herself fading, falling back into the shadowed recesses of tavern wall. A pull on her soul brought back into the moment and she rose to her feet, enough was enough.

The man knew of her thoughts and his expression of jollity ceased. Looking to them both he raised a hand in signal to those who awaited their catch.

Five guards rushed across the tavern and to the young couple.

Watching both be dragged to the floor before being carried away, the barmaid hid her tears in fear of reprisal, witnessing first-hand the dread penetrating her city and spreading across the land of her birth.

Ignoring the damp and cold piercing the cell's menacing atmosphere her steadfast belief in truth kept her sane.

For three days she had sat there, given water and stale bread each night, a meal she knew was only given to keep her alive and so be able to join the screams of redemption echoing across her lone walls from the mouths of others.

There was only one other she cared for now. Every night she had tried to discern his voice. That identification did not come, making her thoughts multiply in the implications of terrible scenario.

Another day would come to pass until she met with the fears of others, portrayed in the oppression of those of well-meaning and differing views to the norm.

Startled by a turn of key she wakened from what little sleep had been since her arrival.

Candlelight streamed into her awareness and she stared at the two guard's entry into her cell. Each stood aside to reveal the shadow of a single figure walking towards her with no hurry to his footsteps.

His awaited arrival to her displayed luxurious material of mauve coloured cassock from feet to neck where from a tormented body on a cross hung from a gold chain, the one who it was said by the Church paid scorn onto those who did not follow His word.

Towering over her, he stopped her attempt to stand with a hand stretched out in blessing, allowing her weakened state to remain on the patch of rotting straw given as bed.

Disgusted by his act of misguided kindness she stood anyway only to be knocked back to the floor by one of the guard's heavy hands.

Both she and the guard's actions produced a smile on the holy man's lips. Pausing a moment in his satisfaction he then clicked his fingers. Another two guards appeared and she stared at the one they now carried between them.

Fighting back tears she looked to her love, an arm cast across each of the guard's shoulder, head bowed, his bare feet dragging across cold stone flooring.

More candles were brought for her to see clearly. With all her strength she did not shy away, allowing no further delight for those of power.

Riled by her lack of emotion the man of cloth reached for her love's hair and with a yank of brown curls showed her husband's features in fresh candle's flicker.

Her composure faltered in what she saw. Her heart going out to him in seeing the bruised and swollen jawline she had kissed so often. The worst came when she could not see past his swollen eyelids, concealing those green pools with sparks of gold that captivated her so.

As the guards slumped her husband to the floor it took all her might not to rush to the shallow breaths before her. Giving no gratification in such an act she stared up at her inquisitor. It was then the questioning began.

An endless circle of inquiries bombarded her. When talk of healing against the Lord's word came she laughed to the ridiculous ideal of peace she had been told He demonstrates.

That laughter caused her another slap by an overzealous guard keen to look good in his master's view.

Hours passed and each occasion she denied her and her husband's wrong doing, for how could providing comfort for the sick be seen as immoral she had asked, only to receive another guard's palm.

Showing no sign of breaking the holy man used his final tactic. Walking to her husband he raised a handful of hair again. Looking to his victim he then stared to the woman who infuriated him so.

It was then he gave his ultimatum. Telling how he knew one of them was the heretic he searched for he announced the death of whoever it was.

Another tug on curls gave rise to his next statement, that if the one he held now could not talk then it was he who could not defend himself and was so proved guilty.

She took his words. Letting them form within her she knew now of her actions needed to save the one she loved, the one who had been through too much already.

Looking into the inquisitor's eyes she pronounced that it was she who had acted against his beloved church, that is was she who had acted in heresy.

A murmur came from her love. She knew he could not muster the words to say to save her, knowing full well of what was to come.

She nodded to her husband, her stare filled with love before turning with glares of animosity to the ones who now represented the notions of idol monarchy of fancy and trend.

Her defiance aggravated all who had shown brutish traits of the human condition that day. Another click of fingers saw to a raise of arm from the guard nearest.

Looking up to the axe on its descent towards her, a light of pure brightness filled the cell and all motion stopped around her.

"I think we know what is to come," a new voice sounded across damp walls.

Looking to its source she watched a man walk from a once darkened corner. Not understanding why she had not seen him before she stared over to her love.

"And he will be joining you soon also."

Understanding came to her in these moments and she reached for the man's hand now stretched out to her.

"You have suffered too much pain these last days, there is no need for more," he spoke again as she took his palm in hers.

It was only then she let her tears fall.

CHAPTER TEN

Leaving her seat she walked from the table and across the library. Staring up to the growing darkness displayed above she continued until standing at the far end of book filled walls. George remained in his chair, his eyes upon her solitary stance.

A new set of tears fell from her. No sobs came, just a slow cascade of salty drops down delicate cheekbones.

Memories of the one she had read of came to her, or more so the physical description that seemed to fall in line with her own appearance now. Was it that in her lifetimes of womanhood she portrayed the same exterior to others every time?

Her questioning diminished the sadness felt towards reading of those persecuted for their beliefs.

Looking over to George waiting patiently for her, she walked back to him and returned to her seat.

"Better?" George asked on her arrival.

"Yes, I guess," she said, a host of questions burning inside her.

Trying to control her mind she set aside her want for answers as to why the atrocities written had happened, deciding to deal with them after learning of her soul's physicality. This she knew would give her some respite from the ferocity encountered amid the streets of fifteenth century Madrid.

"Do I always look the same?" She asked.

"Do those green eyes you know so well ever change?"

All her answers were reached in George's reply, yet still she did not feel ready to meet with what had been encountered in the last lifetime read.

"But, I am not always a woman," she said. "How do I appear when I live life as a man?"

"Different than you do now," came George's simple reply.

Looking to the smile George now gave she knew it was time to talk of the words that had brought such sorrow to her.

"It was awful," she told him.

"The ending, yes it was. But, can you see beyond the callousness of others? Can you read between the lines as to the situation your life entailed? Think not of the demise shown, but of the traits and relationships held within such times."

Doing her best to forget the horrific last moments that had held such distress within she concentrated on what could link herself to with the lifetime of Spanish origins. As with the other lives uncovered at George's side she searched for memories to bring her answers to the forefront.

"They were both… I was, a doctor," she said.

"Not necessarily,"

"I was a healer, what's the difference?"

George looked in delight to her feisty approach.

"And there is another of your characteristics," he told her.

Blushing to her outburst, she too hid her joy, not only for the amusement caused but once again for the recognition of him knowing her soul so well.

"The difference is only slight," George took the lead. "A fleeting nuance that is as vital as it is constructive."

"They followed their instincts when it came to healing others," she said, her understanding reached in recollections of her own Spanish incarnation's recollections.

"This they did, a tried and tested way so diverse to the usual constructs and conformities of medicinal hierarchy."

"And so they were hunted and persecuted for being different."

"I'm afraid this is exactly why your lifetime came to such an abrupt end."

"Through fear," she whispered, her awareness to the situation pinpointing the reasons for persecution, a fact that confounded her. Weren't all innovations classed as different and new in their first conception and following introduction to the world?

A want to explore these foresights came to her, but first she knew she must air the other observation held in the reading of Spain's religious oppressions.

"We were together again," she said "We spent another lifetime together, although it a short one."

"And what did you perceive in the bonds you held with one another?"

Closing her eyes, warm emotions flowed over her, experiencing the feelings and attributes of the couple who sought an escape from the tyranny of others.

"Tell me what you sense," George spoke softly to her. "Speak to me of the emotions which surround you now."

"The comfort of another," she said, her eyes still closed. "Safety, I feel safe being in the presence of the soul with the green eyes. At ease also, as if… As if it is meant to be."

"And of what came to pass? What do you sense from those who castigated you for your beliefs?"

Wanting to stay nestled within the warm memories of the soul she became whole when with, her eyes opened, her expression changing from one of bliss to that of resentment. An overriding loathing of her persecutors appeared, as did the stench of fear flowing from them and towards her and her love.

"Fear," she said. "Each one of them was bathed in it, fear that slithered its way through each soul, leaving its mark, bringing torment to others who did not obey the same rules as they."

"And where do you think that fear arrived from?"

George's question reach deep inside her heart. She knew the answers, her fire and passion bringing them forth in a torrent of words.

"Their souls were young. They knew no different. They were so caught up in their own beliefs that there was little room to consider another's ideas."

"And of the wrath they aroused within you, not only now but then in your life spent as a fierce Spanish healer. What happened as you began to understand they knew not what they did?"

Her manner calmed in George's changing direction of questioning. Aware the anger burning within her heart had faded, her thoughts towards those who had inflicted such harm on her and her loved one fell into the absolution her soul craved for.

"With forgiveness comes great strength," George took her hand in his.

"I see this. I feel it," her fingers wrapped around his as another tear escaped her.

"Forgiveness with understanding."

"Compassion," she echoed his soft tones.

"As you have spoken of already, those who inflict pain on others are seldom aware of their actions. They run blind to the devastation they cause."

"And the fear in them is fuelled by terror of being seen as different, and so they project their own insecurities of being found out onto others." Breaking free of George's hand, her passionate disclosure brought renewed strength to her heart as she continued. "Fear of those who are courageous enough to walk a path unlike the one looked upon as being a more conventional route."

Watching her calm once more in the compassion that had taken centuries to attain, George settled back. His blue eyes looked into hers.

"Can you find any redemption within the story you have just read?" He asked. "Was there a single act that shone bright with optimism within the confines of such wastefulness of life?"

With his stare continuing on her, he waited for answers to come.

Not shying away from George's gaze, her mind re-entered the final moments lived as a Spanish healer who was executed for believing in what was seen as being outside customary ways.

As if present in the dungeons of central Madrid, the dampness of air hung around her. She could hear the screams of others in a similar predicament as her own and of course she could see her love, his eyes closed tight, the green and gold flecks she yearned to see concealed from her, and so she continued watching all play out before her up until the moment George had stepped in to take her away from what was to be the most abruptness of endings.

It was in these final moments her answers were found. A reclamation of goodness retrieved within the callousness of the unaware and fearful.

"Sacrifice," she said, her mind at last leaving the place of misery where such a virtue had appeared.

"A moment of beauty found amid a sea of inhumanity."

"I gave my life for my love. I sacrificed all so he could continue."

"Of that you did."

"But, it was all in vain. The inquisitors told me this before you came to get me."

"It does not matter the outcome, it is your decision that holds the baring."

"How?"

George saw her interest was piqued. This came of little surprise having seen her expression of curiosity dance before him over the centuries, both in her guise of attractive woman with the finest of cheekbones and as the dark haired young man who would also frequent this very library asking of the one with green eyes he would encounter from time to time.

"If a selfless decision is reached then it does not matter if said act is instigated or not. If the mere thought is true and of genuine virtue then that is enough."

"Enough for what?"

"Enough to be reciprocated in future lifetimes to come."

"Then my sacrifice will be rewarded in another lifetime, by another soul?"

"Yes."

"So, if true intentions to do good is there yet not carried out, the results are the same."

"Yes," George nodded to her, waiting for her next line of questioning.

"How? Will someone make a sacrifice for me?"

Seeing his words acted out before her once more, her return to the imaginings of dungeon and all present caused a secondary realisation to appear.

"And if a soul's act was a bad one?"

"Then this too will come back on them."

"Even if they didn't carry it out, even if they just thought it?"

"Yes. If their thought of doing harm to another is with genuine intent, then yes, the same repercussions are present."

Leaning back in her chair she looked upwards to the library's window and to the stars that had multiplied in count over the last few chapters read.

Finding solace in the grandeur of distant galaxies near and far, she mulled over the connotations of good and bad thoughts towards others. Implications realised, entwined in George's comforting presence as he guided her from lifetime to lifetime via the pages of a book.

Her view left the stars to their own devices and she looked to George.

"Another?" She reached for the next chapter page, her heart resting in confidence that the lifetime now to be discovered held more brightness than the last.

CHAPTER ELEVEN

Florence
The Principate of Tuscany
1503AD

Always surprised by the size of the studio, she walked across empty white marbled flooring towards drawn curtains. Feeling the warmth of an early summer's morning enticing more heat into the room she drew back the veil holding sunlight at bay.

Rich Tuscan light filled the studio, preparing its build through the day from midday's blanket of pure whiteness to an imminent display of yellows and ambers until finally submitting to the deepening orange and reds of dusk.

For many years she had done the same most mornings. The simple joy of watching sunrays fall across her workplace each day brought an understanding of what her master must see in his visions beyond all others.

She too made preparations for the day ahead. Disrobing from her street clothing she cared not if those who had entered the studio on her arrival now saw her naked. Had not the kings and queens of Europe seen her body also, and so did most days in the capture of her likeness.

Watching those setting up easels and tables filled with still fresh oil paints of all colours imagined, she closed her eyes for a moment and breathed in the scents of linseed and walnut, before looking over to glass jars containing shelled remnants of both, fascinated by her master's want for perfection in the preparation of oils added to small powdered hills of nature's varied pigments.

Dressing in the loose white linin tunic preferred by the one always sat for, she remembered his discovery of her three years previously stood outside Florence's famed hall of worship.

Each day she would walk through Florentine streets in dawn's first light. Taking in the sights and sounds of her city awakening she would often pause before the basilica of Santa Croce.

Amazed by its beauty she would study the morning's primary sunbeams strike columns and reliefs with soft touches of ochre. On occasions if time allowed she would enter onto sacred grounds to marvel at what lay within.

Her visits though were always cut short in her want to leave the citadel. It was not the surroundings which gave rise to such brief stays, of this she knew on discovering the paintings of blues and whites held within. There was something else that played on her heart, a wanting to escape the echoed footsteps and mumbles of scripture that greeted her and to explore more of the world outside. Walking from the central doorway beneath a high defined symmetrical archway that morning she had looked out pensively over the square before her.

Ignoring the attention her fine beauty always produced, a calm voice had caught her unawares.

Turning to the old man, a sense of nothing but peace and kindness settled about him. Her agreement for his request to paint her came in an instant of mention, for she knew who had now approached her. Having studied his work for the majority of her twenty-four years, she felt safe with this stranger who was to become a friend, confidant and inspiration. She was also aware her unique beauty would not be taken advantage of, it being common knowledge his desires lay elsewhere.

With first preparations made throughout the studio her view fell to the view of Florence so few had seen from such lofty heights. Always aware of the privileged position she held amongst other artist's models, she had decided from her first sitting that he would be the only one she would sit for, so fortifying her role to him as muse.

Silence descended on all present as their master entered his work place. With a nod to all he waited for them to leave but for the one he felt so protective over. It was she he saved a smile for.

Not a word was spoken between the two as each took to their place, he behind his easel, she stood facing its small wooden panel, its imagined contents waiting to be discovered.

Wanting his attention she made do with the momentary peaks towards her, assuming the pose she somehow knew was needed.

The beginnings of a new painting always brought with it some tension. This stress would fade as planned sketches of browns and white were made in the weeks preceding commencement.

On her walk to the studio that morning she recognised he was ready to commit to painting, a special day for them both.

A morning's work completed both retired for lunch. A time looked forward to most. This was not from want of movement for her lithe body craved, nor for the olives and other delicacies each would share within the midday shadows of the studio's balcony. What truly was her delight lay in the allowance of being shown the work produced that morning.

She was always surprised such an act came in the time spent with him. Tales other artist's models told of those who painted them were lost to her. Never had she witnessed a throwing of brush nor had tantrums of creative temperament cast in her direction for the slightest of movements that may have occurred. This only added to the joy of being within the presence of genius.

Granting her attendance with a nod she walked to see the openings of the new painting. Standing behind the old man she peered closer. The toned torso and small touch of hip she was so proud of were nowhere to be seen. Only her pensive expression and slight of neck appeared across what had once been polished wooded grain. Her eyes followed delicate lines of jaw and cheek, finding solace in the deep browns used to evoke each stroke.

On looking to the one who had produced such beauty his white beard raised in smile to her reaction before he rose and directed her to their awaiting feast overlooking a Florentine skyline.

Falling into their routine over the next two days each fulfilled their duties, yet this would change on the fourth morning of her portrait's conception.

A usual stop taken before Santa Croce was cut short that morning. A sense of urgency pushed the artist's model onwards. With a knowing as to why her footsteps now carried her with haste she relinquished her wants of seeing granite's amber glow and continued.

On arrival to the studio she was greeted by only one of the many who would perform their daily chores. Explanations followed as to the reasons behind their master's absence that day.

In knowledge of his duties towards the son of Pope Alexander VI and his duties as military architect, it was of no surprise that an occasional day would be missed at his easel.

As her messenger left under her instruction she remained in the studio and with eyes closed inhaled the scent of the previous day's paints.

Staying to see the mid-morning sunlight she studied the development of her portrait. It seemed strange that no colour had been added and that the piece retained its primary sketch appearance.

Wondering how she would fill her day she made to leave. She stopped at the studio door.

Looking to her side she saw a pile of newly stretched canvas, its wooden frames bearing the force of taught craftsmanship.

Next to white starched rectangles, leftover oil paints from weeks passed remained. With thoughts racing she stepped to them and reached out her hand.

The slight film over each colourful mound split beneath her touch allowing soft pastes to emerge. Of that moment she knew what she must do.

Answering the calls her heart had made yet had been kept hidden, she soon sat before her master's spare easel, a small blank canvas and remnants of paint brought to life with dabs of rich walnut oil at her side.

Never once had she mentioned her urge to create. A smile came to her in those moments, one not only of joy, but in the wonder of the position to where she would make her first strokes of dreams onto the empty space placed before her.

Choosing a colour with one of the old paintbrushes she had recovered from the corner of the studio she leant forwards as she had watched her peer do so many times before and placed a daub of phthalo blue to the top of the canvas' left hand corner. Surprise caught her to the vibrations of the brush handle on contact with staunch, tight material.

Another stroke came and then another, her playful touches revealed by overwhelming tenacity as she continued, her solitary stance amplified in the emerging scene in front of her soul.

Lost in her elation and sometimes torment she did not notice dusk's approach until a voice spoke out to her. Turning to the tones always loved, her expression of apology lessened in the joy her master now held.

Without a word he pulled a chair up beside her and both looked to her naïve reproduction of blue sky, sand strewn coastline and low cliff top, her heart beating fast with every small nod and murmur produced beside her.

Following that day after displaying her passions in oil, nothing changed in their morning routine and ritual of artist and model. It was the afternoons that now took on a different role.

So enamoured by the natural talent presented to him on his return from duties beyond his control, the old master encouraged his muse to continue her artistic pursuits and when lunch was over she would set up an easel and paints in the studio and continue her joy as her master slept.

On his awakening hours later, together they would sit and debate methods of blending and the qualities of light and shade until as one year passed talk of composition entered the field.

Her skills developed under his watchful eye. Little tuition was given as it was deemed for her to discover through trial and error, an ideal she would come to appreciate in the years that followed.

Her main passion was for flowers and the reproductions made of petal and stem were often shrouded in colours of brightness, yet there was another theme that would reoccur in those happy afternoons of being allowed to perform with brush in hand.

This prompted great delight in her master, he too holding a love for the seas of the world and the challenges given in capturing them on canvas.

Other themes came with frequency into her work alongside seas of blue. Creations of vast snow laden landscapes played a part, as did the depiction of ships of friend and foe arriving on beaches of sand and shale.

Religion took its form also on canvas. Many times she would capture dawn's light settled across Santa Croce's stonemasoned facer, adding a solitary monk into her compositions from time to time.

The trend of holy imaginations continued where she once attempted the portrayal of Spanish orthodoxy. This canvas however was discarded before finished, having evoked a sadness within her which was contained in each brushstroke made. This sorrow of which she could not understand came again on her attempt of portraiture of a young Spaniard, leaving the piece unfinished but for the outlines of brown curls and finer details of eyes of green.

Continuing with visions of flowers and seascapes one thing came to pass as a result of her release in oils.

The portrait of her that was kept in the browns and whites of early sketch, completed days after she had revealed her artistic flare, held a stare she would never embrace again. The pensive longing her master had captured was gone from her now, released in the passion found amongst paintbrush and oils.

Memories of those happy times would return to her over the coming years, even in the sadness following the passing of her master, tutor and friend on French soil.

In his memory she had painted the night skies she would gaze upon for inspiration, becoming the first female artist of the Renaissance period to do so. Her depiction of the cosmos and its trail of star and galaxy was received with much acclaim and so began her career as a respected artist in her own right.

The rewards of her labour provided many delights, yet there was one such pleasure that always alluded her in that there was no-one to share her spoils with. In this she dived into her artistic pursuit of perfection with vigour, finding comfort amid the scent of linseed and dried pigment.

As her years in Florence passed she looked to Santa Croce's tall walls for answers in her want to leave the city of her birth.

One morning on looking to familiar tinges of orange play over stone pillars she recalled talk of a similar yet softer light. One that belonged to the southern city she had always wanted to visit, Naples.

Frequent trips resulted from that day to a source of new light for her paintings. Those moments of pleasure taken on board ship added a host of new concepts to her on riding the surf of the Ligurian sea whilst looking out to her homelands western coastlines.

As she gained in age those voyages became much harder. A decision had to be made and so one day she left the Florentine streets of her youth and found herself a home in the city she had loved since her first arrival to the harbour on the Gulf of Naples.

Making herself a home, she bought three buildings sat next together in a row overlooking the seas she treasured.

With renovations completed she enjoyed the space given by knocked down wall and ceiling. With a studio filled with the light craved for most of all she cherished her bedroom. Made from three previous rooms, she had positioned her bed in view of the sea, but her delight came in the skylight above her pillow, where laying at rest and she could watch the string of stars dissecting the night sky passing over her. It would be on the eve of her seventy-fourth birthday that she would revel in the peace found upon those shores.

Resting back on her pillow she stared up to the developing stars above, the smells of a new painting from studio below drifting up on her prompting memories of days passed. Leaving her bed she soon returned with the two artworks instigating such recollections.

Climbing back onto her bunk she looked to the unfinished painting from years ago. Never understanding why she could never return to finishing the piece, her finger edged gently around the depiction of such stunning eyes and to the beginning brushstrokes of brown curls framing the features of the young man of Spain.

Putting the piece aside she then held her prized possession in her hands, the wooden panel of mastery that meant so much.

Looking to the young features displayed across its front in browns and white, she remembered the moment her master had given it to her on her twenty-sixth birthday. Each year on the night before her anniversary she would study the work of her master's hand. On every occasion she marvelled at the beauty she had once held.

Resting back, her head light, she placed her portrait of youth on her lap and stared up to pinpoints of light forming above her, finding solace from her memories of the how young she had once appeared.

"And so you shall you again," a voice spoke out to her.

No fear came to her in those moments, only comfort.

"And so shall you be old again," the voice continued. "For this is the cycle all pass through. The way of how things are."

A nod came from the former artist's model who had achieved so much in one lifetime.

Looking to the paintings of her youth and that of the unknown man for a final time, with a faint smile she reached for her visitor's hand as her bedroom filled with rich, white light as soothing as a Tuscan dawn.

CHAPTER TWELVE

On reading George's closing words to the woman who had lived a life filled with the joys of creativity she stood once more as she had done after completing the previous chapter. This time her emotions held a different taste.

Looking to George she left his side and walked to the doorway that had granted both of them entrance into the vast library and stepped outside.

She raised her hand and dissected the line of ever growing stars with her finger, an act she now knew had been carried out many lifetimes before.

Resting her arm back at her side she glanced over to the bush that had proved so significant in her understanding of her position. It's once display of petals had gone and all that remained was a maze of stick and branch now transformed into nightfall's sheens of dark blues and black, prompting her to try and discern how long she had been at George's side. This proved difficult, she was just here, she understood that, another acceptance that seemed to ease her path.

Turning back to the library her attention fell to the ornate bench placed at its front overlooking the seascape that had always offered her such mystery and enticement. Within moments she was seated, legs outstretched, her view held on highlighted waves, listening to the soothing crash each one made seconds after arrival onto sand and shale.

Settling into her new setting her thoughts returned to the lifetime discovered as an artist's model and artist in their own right.

It was not just the life led that absorbed her now, it was how all that had gone before appeared to come together in the telling of the tale.

So many factors had been presented to her that her choice to leave the library seemed the only way in which to digest the significance of each aspect uncovered within that lifetime of the Italian Renaissance.

From her cliff edge seat she watched the far horizon's faint glow and looked to the silver gleam cast across surrounding bracken landscapes. Recalling the browns and ochre now masked by darkness of night, her thoughts called upon the painting that had always captivated her.

Could it have been true? That the small wooden panel which held such beauty was in fact the rendition of her former self from half a millennia ago? This she knew was only the first of several facets that linked each lifetime read so far within her book's glowing pages.

Trying to piece all clues together she closed her eyes as to gain some peace of mind. With only the distant sound of rolling wave accompanying her, she summoned the calmness she was aware would be needed to unravel what had unfolded before her.

Sitting in stillness her soul reached for that which had come to pass. Recapping all discovered, the icy tundra of mankind's infancy ran onto British seas and into waters found on the coastlines of warmer climes. Great citadels of artistic merit filled her senses, Mediterranean vistas which lead her back to the words that had prompted her arrival to the bench overlooking beachhead, sky and sea.

Opening her eyes, ready to continue, she looked up to the night sky before making back into the library, keen to talk of the moments encountered with George and to bask in the comfort found at his side.

Taking another look at the increasing star trails which always seemed to play an important part in her journey through each lifetime she stood and walked to the library entrance, her spirit reinvigorated and ready for the answers George would invite her to find.

"Here she is," George smiled on her return.

Taking her seat next to him once more his greeting was returned with refreshed curiosity and eager want of what was to be revealed.

"I see you are more than ready to continue."

"I am," her reply came and she turned to him. "That was me," she said, a mix of pride and astonishment in her tone, "the painting, it was me."

"It was."

"And the other painting..." Her words trailed from her, experiencing an upset she knew would surface in confronting the composition of a former love. "Those eyes, I didn't know why then but now I see the heartache harboured within me was too strong to finish his portrait, even though those emotions were buried and left unknown deep in my heart."

"This is true also. Now you can see what remains important to you. What aspects of each lifetime carry with you into the next?"

"Like my traits?"

"It is not only how your soul is, what characteristics are prevalent to you, but also situations, locations and other people."

"Is that why as an artist's model and artist I felt drawn to the Cathedral I had spent time in as a monk?"

"Locations of the past are often encountered again, memories of times spent in certain places around the world can draw a soul to want to be within that environment once more. To be stood in places no matter how far away from where they were born, so they may experience the same emotions and feelings they did there in a life lived sometimes centuries before."

Her hands returned to the book and leafed back through its pages.

George watched her search, awaiting her to discover all in her own time.

Reading over words already seen, her view left the book and to George. As ever he awaited her approach to him, letting her form her own questions as new insights to the world and lives lived within came to her.

"I can see all these connections so clearly now," she said.

"And of those you encounter?"

The kindly stares of the one who had guided her former self in the art of oil on canvas came to her. Picturing herself sitting next to him in a sunlit Florence studio, she wondered if they had met before and if they would again in the pages to follow.

"Some come to us late," George knew of who she thought of now. "Visiting our lives when the time is right, helping us forwards in our learning of the ways of the world."

"Is this what happened to me? He arrived to show me how and that I can paint?"

George smiled to her. "Not every lifetime is filled with those we grow accustomed to meeting with. On some occasions though, there appears a soul who joins with another along their path, sometimes guiding sometimes simply accompanying."

Memories of feeling the old man's presence returned to her. Recollections of guidance and deep friendship played upon her heart and so reaching new understandings to George's teachings.

"Others have helped me also?" She said.

"Of course. Can you remember another who helped your soul? One who encouraged the wants he saw inside your heart, giving you the impetus to continue forwards in your own way?"

She looked to the book in hope her answer would appear in glowing letters as did its leather bound covers hold.

"Think of your previous chapter's locations," George instructed. "Who gave such guidance there?"

Within moments of George's prompt she knew of where he spoke. The grand front of Florence's Basilica di Santa Croce filled her mind, and the monk of close to two hundred years earlier who she had represented on canvas. This led her to think of the one who had shown such kindness and guidance towards the one depicted on those holy steps.

"The old friar, he gave me the book," she said, her eyes widening to her discovery.

"And so he sent you on the journey he saw your soul needed to take."

"Yes, he did," her joy overflowed in her words. "Now I will never hold a fear to me again."

"Why not?"

"Because now I know such souls exist, that such hearts filled with kindness are destined to meet with me once again."

She held her silence, swathed within her new found knowledge, enjoy the comfort she now was aware would come to her in further lifetimes. Added wellbeing came as she glanced over to George. This time it was she who reached out and took his hand in hers.

"And you will be here also. Every time, so you may show me all these treasures you unveil to me on each occasion between lifetimes."

George gave her hand a squeeze in confirmation of her words.

"I am ready to read onwards," she smiled to him and reached for the book.

Finding the start of her next chapter she took a moment to consider what had been talked of since reading of the artist's model of Florence.

Seeing the monk represented in oils as he stood outside the tall walls of Florence's basilica, her soul met with the rendition of her former self. Her head shook from side to side as she began to see the complexity of threads in time as each of her lifetimes progressed onwards.

Thinking of those last moments in the New York studio looking to the small wooden board that displayed her image, she imagined her laughter to the notion that the beautiful pensive stares of browns and amber were in fact her from half a century ago. So too, she knew her laughter would have been produced in those times had someone pointed out that the monk portrayed in detailed brush strokes was in fact her two hundred previous to then.

Of the fact that each incarnation had shared the same location beneath her much loved spray of stars on the Tuscan coastlines each had adored, the same retort of sceptic giggles she was sure would have sufficed also.

Returning to her book she paused once more as a new concept came to her.

George watched her scan the books of others all around them, aware she now considered how many times she featured within those pages.

"And so also are your deeds represented there," he told her.

"As with the one who had taught me to paint?"

"Yes, and as with the one with green eyes also."

"They search for me too?" She asked, surprised at never entertaining such ideas.

"Of course," George. As do they all the same way you do also. Yet no disappointment is held in not seeing you, for they know the way of things.

They know how they will one day be in your company again, as do you know you shall find a similar comfort with them also, wherever that may be."

Mulling over his words, more insights came to her, expanding the already complex links and attachments that fuelled her curiosity with every turn of page.

George laughed aloud as she slumped down in her chair beside him.

"So much to keep up with," she said to him.

"And this is a reason why a soul does not retain all its memories for every life journey taken."

George's statement answered her next line of questioning as to why she could not recall such important matters. In a way she found her temporary amnesia a blessing. This not only meant she could read on with ease and be able to enjoy her lifetimes afresh, it also gave an element of surprise as to what and who she would meet with next.

"Shall we?" She leant to the book once more. "Japan," she read the next chapters opening location aloud, her heart eager to discover what had once been.

CHAPTER THIRTEEN

Edo, Japan
1603AD

Morning skies greeted the ones who in turn had welcomed boats laden with Pacific hauls hours before dawn.

These first rays of sun always signalled a much needed break for the gutters and skilleters of Edo Bay.

Leaving their work to congregate around market vendors that had descended on the fish market's gates, bowls of steamed rice and hot soy bean were ready on demand to appease a worker's hunger.

Watching her co-workers leave to satisfy their needs, as was usual she did not join them in their feast. Putting the knives of her trade on the board before her she walked towards the waters which provided all the company required.

Reaching the place she would always sit she looked down to her smock's hem. Its salty bleached white edging of frayed material fell over the heavy ankle boots that gave as much pain to her feet as did the indignity of having to wear them.

Changing her view to the gentle lap of western Pacific reaches, a respite from her work came as it always did, bringing solace in her daily choice to sit alone whilst others ate and laughed.

It had been her decision and hers alone not to accompany those working at her side through darkness and the eventual blue sky of morning.

The option to sit in solitude had been a wise one, of this she was sure in knowledge of the fiery temperament possessed. In all her twenty-two years it had always been the same.

Seabirds swooped down into her view, each one snatching remnants of highly prized blue fin tuna from the ocean surface tainted with pink tinged surf. She thought how these birds showed little grace in their actions and raised a smile recalling the same applied to those she kept from now.

Considering the reasons held behind her self division from others, once again this confirmed her want to sit alone, away from the advances of men and the snide remarks of women, both reactions focused on the unique beauty she held.

This inherited affliction so many wished for caused the isolation she at times experienced. Preferring a solitary existence to the relentless attention of others, her own feistiness and quick retorts played a part in her own self-contained world, aware of the trouble her wit could cause from passed experiences of hapless admirers and jealous wagging tongues.

The sound of a familiar bell signalled her time alone was over and so a return to the wolves baying for a piece of what nature had provided her.

Walking by stacks of freshly cut tuna steaks piled high besides pallets of unsavoury looking marine life of all shapes and sizes sharp knives awaited her reappearance. Her footfalls faltered in seeing the stern brow of the market's manger standing at her board.

With brief and curt instructions she was told to report to his office where a man anticipated her arrival. Making her way between the fish market workers pausing from their work she refused to bow her head and instead held her chin high between the leers and sneers sent her way from both sexes.

Any nervousness towards her unexpected meeting faded on her welcome by the man who had called for her. That anxiety disappeared totally as he greeted her with a bow and a smile which made his white beard rise upwards.

Looking to her salt laced trim he shook his head and told her that this very moment she must leave this place behind and accompany him into the city so they may talk better.

Something within her trusted the older man before her and with no hesitation they walked away from Edo's harbour front markets, never to return again.

Going with the gentle demands of her companion she submitted to his wants. Feeling safe in his company as never experienced before she was in awe how within their brief time together she had allowed someone into her solitary world.

Their morning was spent on streets walked so many times before, only now she was inside the shops she had peered into and had wished to enter.

Not questioning the clothes the man chose for her, those answers she knew would come. Adorning the kimono of deep blues she admired his taste in picking such a colour, one which matched her jet black shoulder length hair admirably.

So the morning progressed until those inevitable reasons for his kindness towards her came over a lunch of olives and delicacies from foreign lands she had read of yet never encountered.

First telling of his concerns in seeing her solitary stance when visiting Edo's fish market only days earlier, he then subtly told of the beauty witnessed upon her, his words soft in knowledge of the sometimes harm the afflictions of attraction can bring a soul.

Such was his way with explanation towards his arrival and want of meeting her, she fell into the comfort produced in such little time between them.

Talk of her life story ensued, of her abandonment on the streets of Edo at ten years old. With sympathetic ear the man listened intently as she continued, telling of the work found on the harbour fish market until this day.

Her story complete he paused before revealing the box of surprises he had to offer her.

Listening with as much vigour as he had her, she tried to disguise her excitement to the life now proposed. A life only dared dreamt of.

Midday advanced into the early evening, filled with details of what was to ensue, should his proposition be accepted.

And so, as dusk began to form, they left the table over which her new beginnings had been confirmed, as had the friendship between the two, and they walked together through soft lit Edo streets in preparation for their passage to Kyoto.

Kyoto, Japan
1606AD

Kyoto's late afternoon sun stroked easy across autumn leaves of red and yellow. While some remained on the tree they had grown, all were soon to join those fallen above maple tree root.

Gentle breezes caught the tails of browning leaves, initiating them to shuffle towards the shores of the Kamo River, a rustle which caused the attention of a solitary figure sat on its banks.

Looking back to the Kitayama Mountains overseeing the city's temples and shrines, her view left snow-capped peaks and returned back to the slow torrents in front of her.

Immersed in private thought, it was not that she chose to sit away from prying eyes still encountered, so similar to the ones in her days on Edo's waterfront which gave her reasons for seclusion. Not now after three years spent within Kyoto's walls. It was simply that she enjoyed her own company, enjoyed the moments held alone, observing all around her that at times gave the sense of being invisible in her absence of others.

Neither was it that she was alone. The friendships made with others also of her chosen career of shirabyoshi and odoriko, the hostesses of beauty who danced and performed for the wealthiest clients of Kyoto's aristocracy, were as true to her as she was to them. Then of course there was the one who had initiated her arrival into this world, her devotion to him replicated in the protectiveness he showed towards her.

Over the three years there had been a development in her soul, a paradox held in the admiration for the beauty that had grown since her arrival.

In time she had come to accept the uniqueness her features gave and so the emotional pains of constant attention worried her no more. All this had been brought about in the company of those who held such fine cheekbone and grace. A realisation that the beauty of an individual truly resided in the heart and their actions therefore made.

Her return to moments alone became more frequent. This decision was made once more by choice. She was tired. Not tired in a way that would disturb her attractiveness, it would take much more to take that away, weariness had touched her soul, its grasp upon her tightening by the day.

For weeks following her identification of the fatigue of her inner self on the banks of Kamo River, she continued entertaining the rich clientele who fell under her spell of music and talk, her skills of sharp retort accepted with the charming smile which would follow each occasion of barbed words.

Her friend and confidant who had introduced her to the world of satisfying others in easy jest recognised her tiredness also, their closeness seeing through hidden emotions. It would not be until the last weeks of winter when he would broach the subject with her.

So much was said in their moments of lunchtime feasts, a time together both had always enjoyed. Explanations of her soul's predicament understood by the man she cared so much for.

Saddened by her want of departure, his admiration for her surpassed all his wants for her to remain, shown in the unconditional feelings he had held towards her since their first meeting on Edo's waterfront.

Having seen a similar fatigue happen upon others of such an emotionally taxing profession there was something else he recognised in the young woman sat before him.

The tenacity of spirit he had first acknowledged within her had arisen from the tale of the strength needed in succeeding to live on the city streets, alone and without support. This he was also aware provided an answer to the bouts of the solitary characteristic she carried, a result of which he was sure stemmed from those days.

With these thoughts in mind his want for her to stay grew, knowing how fortunate it was to have been allowed into her private domain.

The compassion and unrestricted love contained for her had surprised his heart, his occupation at times giving insight into the worst possible grounds of the human condition.

This perception of the weariness within a life yet to be lived reminded him of his own approaching years. He had lived, yes, and so his retirement was soon to arrive, but the one who poured her heart out to him now had so much more to do, so much more to experience, so much more to enjoy.

That day her happiness became a priority to him and he was determined to find a way to release her from her contract, an agreement that seemed bound in chains within the ornate chambers of which she now plied her trade.

It took all his influence of a lifetime of good standing to convince those to loosen their hold on an asset of such importance. So had been her success within the night-time hours of the rich and powerful, her skills had always been in demand.

The turning point to the allowance of release was contained in two acts of reasoning.

The first was of the predominant fear held by the beautiful, that the gift handed to them should fade in time, leading them to be replaced by another whose youth, beauty and grace fulfilled the obligations they once met with.

Although she was still young her looks had not faltered in age, it was the second of causes that truly provided her freedom, as it was known from vast experience, that the holding of a weariness of the soul would soon show in the stares of its afflicted, no matter how stunning those eyes they may be.

Plans were made for her leaving in the middle of the year's first month, with Hiroshima seen as ideal for the wants of new career she had spoken of over lunch on her announcement of planned departure.

The farewells she gave to the women she had worked beside within banquets large and small touched her heart in the unconscious feeling she held for all, yet nothing had prepared her for the sadness felt in saying goodbye to the one who had not only given a life, but had also seen to the allowance of her want of living another.

The one who had guided her through the etiquettes and protocols of Kyoto had shown her another place as well, the opening of her heart to others, of which she knew she would eternally be grateful, vowing to do the same for another one day also.

Hiroshima, Japan
1655AD

Waiting patiently she watched the last sightseers leave. Looking to the cherry blossoms all had come to see, there remained the inner delight she had experienced in witnessing the joy of other, yet another hidden pleasure lay in her heart, now she had the displays of Hanami to herself.

This shortest of blooms that at times could be blown away before started in early Springtime winds always delivered happiness to her soul, a place as with the gardens in which she now sat had been cultivated over the years.

Leaning back onto her favoured maple blossom tree, she breathed in the faint yet still present scent of plum tree flower and looked to the pond's tranquill waters ahead.

Watching the koi carp that had been her focus for over forty years, she paid attention to the gentle lap of surf play onto pond banks before looking to the easel and paints set out between her and her beloved waters.

The outline of orange koi swam proud on her canvas, just one mastered brush stroke made to produce its form. Now what remained were the fine details that would explore the carp's true essence, brought together in the prelude of dusk.

Breaking from her want to continue she settled back on the tree trunk that had held her safe and secure for decades and took in the scene around her.

Nothing had changed since her first arrival to the secluded walled garden in the centre of Hiroshima, but for its popularity over the years.

This mattered her little, for she had come to enjoy the brief hellos encountered by those passing by the artist of the koi as he had come to be known.

The short red bridge and its simple design stayed the same except for its annual repainting, as did the pagoda on the island it spanned towards. Her view fell to the row of stepping stones for those wishing to access further small islands of miniature tree and shrub.

Memories of these stones zigzagging through the pond like floating granite disks caused a smile for the one who had loved to step from one to the other on each visit made with her, his white beard lifting upwards in the joy held, not only for his choice to take his retirement from overseeing and finding the shirabyoshi of Kyoto, but for the sheer pleasure of who he spent his time with in his fading years.

She too had treasured these times, his passing bringing a grief unknown before to her, yet an understanding that they would meet once more in another lifetime, as she was sure they had in previous ones already passed.

Her concentration returned to the painting yet to be completed.

Reaching for her brush she paused and wondered of the fatigue she now experienced.

Knowing the painting could wait a little longer in what daylight hours remained her recollections continued.

Within months of arrival to Hiroshima, she had secured a small home for herself from the purse earned in her three Kyoto years.

Settled into that home, days later she began that of which she had wished for, buying easel, canvas and paints so she may begin her hidden passion. In secret she had studied the paintings of Kyoto's temples and galleries, never speaking of her love of art. Starting with flowers her proficiency grew in the depictions made until a new challenge was sought.

Combining her love of Hiroshima's gardens, she took her work outside to capture the beauty contained within quiet walls. Adept at doing so also, her tenacious soul searched for another avenue to stretch her skills. This came in the koi carp meandering through the ponds of her sanctuary.

At first it had been a battle to paint the ever moving creatures. This is where her true artistic talent came into play on realising that it was not the likeness she was meant to capture, but the essence and metaphor of the present moment. With such work beginning to be recognised, her fame grew in her depiction of life with no inclination for neither past nor future.

By the time her friend of white beard and aged years came to live on the same quite street as she that fame had grown. Together they would laugh how the clients she had once entertained still paid her way, only this time it was in the expensive purchase of her paintings which hung upon the walls of the rich and powerful of not just Kyoto, but of Edo and Hiroshima too.

Memories of such laughter left some sorrow on her, only to fade once more in her anticipation of seeing him again in lifetimes to come.

Tiredness revisited her once more. So different she thought now from the weariness that had affected her soul in younger days, which had disappeared on stepping forwards into a new beginnings of Hiroshima's quiet beauty.

The pond, red bridge and unfinished canvas of pond and simple koi body fell from her view as her eyes closed.

They opened again on hearing the voice beside her.

"It is time," the voice whispered.

The man looked at her canvas and then to her frowns. He laughed to what he knew she thought now.

"You shall have time to finish so many more paintings," he told her, his hand stretching out to hers.

Understanding his words, she gave a final glance to the unfinished piece.

As white light surrounded them both she smiled, realising how the fish of Edo had seen to that start of her life in Kyoto, and now all these years later it was closing with the fish of Hiroshima.

CHAPTER FOURTEEN

"That was my painting."

George's pleasure in watching her recognition of times passed never faltered.

"Yes," he said. "It was."

The threads of time, encounters and happenstance were beginning to intertwine and weave their way into her whole being as understanding came in the labyrinth of experiences now read of.

"Another unfinished piece," she said, her head lowering for a moment lost in the thoughts of one from her lifetime before.

George knew of the one she remembered now.

"And so you recognise your artistry," his soft tones urged her to return from past heartache.

"Yes, I was restoring it when…"

"I arrived," George spoke on hearing her words fade from her.

She became lost in thought once more as the realisations that the job she had battled to secure and loved was gone from her now. Even though what she experienced at George's side and continued to do so amongst the pages of this magical book amazed her, some sorrow remained in her awareness that her life as an art restorer had gone.

"Hold no sadness to such things," George said. "As you have seen, each lifetime holds its own joys. Unique stories that encapsulate all which has gone before, as well as fresh scenarios and encounters."

His words eased her sadness, her want to continue with the book, her book, overrode any need for a return to a life she had engineered for herself. Was it like this on each occasion? Was this how she always felt between lifetimes, sat at George's side reading of what had been lived and loved throughout history's silent march?

Memories of her sitting within her studio came to her. Picturing the aged canvas of delicate outline of koi carp set elegantly in mid motion before her, the world around those recollections began to change. The studio's grey walls and various notes and photos lining them faded, only to be replaced by the gardens in which the canvas had been painted.

Her vision continuing, she watched gentle ripples flow across the pond and under an ornate red bridge spanning waterside and small islands filled with miniature tree and shrub.

The canvas before her displayed its wares, one of such beauty that even though it would remain uncompleted would capture the hearts of others for centuries to come.

A new awareness came to her and she began to take on a deeper acceptance of all now experienced, an understanding reached in the merging of lifetimes shown.

Her return was marked by the smile now held towards George.

"And of that life led," he asked her, "was there one who you had met with before?"

Nodding in answer, she warmed to the remembrance of the one who had shown such compassion to her, as had the same soul done so in his guidance of the arts within a sunlit Florentine studio.

"Yes, he appeared to you again," George confirmed. "But even though you experienced such goodness of spirit and unconditional care towards you, was there not another aspect of your life in Japan that coexisted with such kindness?"

Unsure as to what George suggested she searched within her heart for traits of herself uncovered within each lifetime learned of.

Such moments for the short term eluded her. Going through her Japanese lifetime step by step she envisioned herself amid the bustling fish markets of Edo Bay, her life entertaining the rich and powerful until her thoughts finally came to rest within Hiroshima's tranquil walled gardens, aware that somewhere within these moments her answer lay.

"So much experienced in one lifetime," George encouraged her search for the characteristic never truly brought to light before.

"There was," she agreed. "It was of no wonder that I spent so much time alone."

Her statement produced a new smile in George, his happiness edging her forward into full realisation towards her answer.

"Solitude," she said. "This is was I sought all along."

"You did."

"But why?" Wasn't I lonely?"

"Did you feel lonely?"

Watching her think over his words, George waited once more for her recognitions to come through.

"No," she replied, her voice touched by an element of surprise to her admission. "How could I enjoy my solitude so much and not feel lonely?"

George looked to her, his smile easing the slight anxiety he sensed beginning to rise within her dealing with another foreign concept.

"Solitude," he gathered his words to explain all to the curious soul beside him.

Letting the word settle within her, her heart waited for explanations to further her understanding.

"Solitude is something a soul chooses to experience," he said to her. "Whereas loneliness is something that is imposed on a soul."

"It's as simple as that?"

"In a way, yes. Just this brief description to separate the two states can often aid a soul to understanding the isolation they at times may feel."

"Are some souls not able to see the difference?"

"Occasionally," George said. "You see, sometimes when a soul spends time alone they can often think that they are lonely, that the seclusion they are experiencing has been put upon them, when in reality they have chosen to be alone, yet in the enjoyment found in such a choice some guilt can be produced."

"Guilt?"

"Guilt that the joy found in solitude should not be allowed, that to be alone and so blissfully content is deemed wrong in a world of constant interaction with others."

Recalling her time on the banks of Kyoto's riverside, there held a sense that similar thoughts had once played upon her, as she also suspected had happened to the majority of her previous incarnations.

"Before we can explore solitude," George looked to her. "What does loneliness mean to you?"

Taking a moment she considered the feelings encountered on her first arrival to New York. Her expectations had been met with, this was true in the guise of work, her anticipations granted in the art works she spent time in such privileged proximity with. It had been her social life that had lived below its means.

"I remember those times also," George told her. "But, can you recall the great energy you held then, your eagerness to experience all on the streets and avenues so different to the home of your upbringing?"

"Yes," she lightened. "I remember them very well."

"From an outsider's point of view, the solitude or loneliness of another's soul looks a lot alike. Only the soul itself in question can identify which emotion of solitariness they are experiencing." George leant to her. "And so, which did you feel in those first few weeks of your arrival in a new city?"

Starting to understand the differing states of being alone and the concepts held therefore within, she recalled the smiles she had held when first discovering the city, her solitary lunches spent happily watching the world go by. These memories produced her answers and she smiled to George, who she was certain had joined her on the tours of the new pastures taken she remembered now.

"I wasn't lonely," she told him. "I in fact enjoyed my time alone."

"Of that I watched," George delighted in her awareness. "You felt alive, filled with vigour."

"I did."

"This is because solitude restores the mind, giving it the vitalisation needed to continue its exploration and discovery."

"And loneliness depletes the mind and heart," she said, a smile upon her lips in seeing her statement pleased George so much.

"Loneliness is such a negative state, its sense of isolation giving the soul a feeling that something is missing, a harsh punishment that can see to the building of discontent and deficiency within the recesses of the soul's core, leading to an estrangement caused in the awareness of excess aloneness."

"Then why is solitude so important?" She asked, wanting to understand the subtle differences being shown to her now.

"Self-induced solitude, or shall we say being alone without being lonely, can lead to self-awareness. When used for reflection, our want for an inner search for growth becomes explored in ways we could never imagine when in the company of others."

"When we are on our own and have chosen to be so, only then are we truly our own selves," she said.

"And so this leads to the discovery of who a soul really is, which can lead to discovering their wants and desires and ultimately give an insight in how to achieve such dreams."

Recollections of all the lifetimes she had read of came to her in forms of the moments she had spent alone. Settling into her memories she saw those moments roll out before her, the solitary walk across the snow laden landscapes of man's early ancestry transformed into the old doctor's lone march on her quest to aid those of warfare, those footsteps soon turned into ones belonging to the French knight on his often solo treks across Africa's northern shores. So her memories continued taking the same figure devoid of race or sex across the annuls of time, through Italy's fourteenth and sixteenth centuries until arriving at the lithe silhouette of a Japanese geisha looking onto the meandering waters of Kyoto's central city river.

She glanced over to George, aware that he too had witnessed her journey in the guises of differing landscapes and bodies. So too was she aware that he also observed her evolving understanding of her true self, realised in each situation she had sought seclusion from others.

"All these moments are yours," George told her. "All these realisations that grow within you on every lifetime lived and completed stay with you."

"And times of solitude are the key," she said, her awareness growing in the ease now surrounding her.

"Yes, those times of quiet reflection and learning are of great significance, yet never forget that in order to learn we must engage with others also."

With these words she put aside remembrances of more solitary times in which peace and serenity had been found, recalling instead the one who for the second time had now helped her on her journey through life.

"Will he help me again?" She asked.

George did not question who she spoke of now. The complexities of what was to prevail in the following chapter would hinder her understanding and he simply motioned to the book laid out on the mahogany surface before them.

Taking his prompt she reached for the book, her finger running beneath its chapter heading of American origins.

CHAPTER FIFTEEN

Salem Town
Massachusetts, USA
1692AD

The call of gulls gathered around the arrival of fishing trailers hung both in the air and on light Atlantic surface swells.

America's heat wave striking its northeastern states only added to the reverent nature the people of Essex County were recognised as holding, beating hot rays of July sun a trial for those who must temper their emotions in the eyes of the Church.

An unusual silence surrounded the fishermen as seabirds continued to dive for morsels of forgotten or unneeded hauls. Not a single cuss came from their lips, a custom almost mandatory for men of the sea.

Heads down, they concentrated on their work, aged hands and lined faces signifying a life led on the shoreline of Salem Town.

Midday sun sustained its unrelenting heat, causing dry salty breezes to flow across the quiet melancholy of the town's harbour front, yet there was one soul who now walked over Salem's wooden jetty whose emotions were laid bare for all to see, her happy disposition seen as an affliction to others of more puritanical views.

Spying between dark stained wooden slats to lapping seas below she smiled to herself once again in feeling the weight of the wicker basket she now carried homewards, its heaviness deemed a triumph swinging in her hand, its contents the result of a fine collection of seaweeds in colours of emerald green and deep purple.

With no disguise of her delight she recalled her father's instructions towards her public smiles, her tenacious spirit caring not if her actions raised suspicion within the small minded factions of her birthplace.

Leaving the harbour behind she strode onwards through her communities main thoroughfare, her head held high showing a confidence unknown in other twenty-one year olds of Salem.

She ignored the eyes she knew now followed her self-assured gait, wondering why others showed such animosity towards those who were different.

One consideration to the acts of others was that they themselves were so fearful of loneliness from the safety of the fold that the attentions of jealousy visited their souls and so woe betides anyone who followed their heart. Her ideas prompted another smile in wondering if they understood the bravery needed to walk one's own path from stifling conformity, and also if they realised the same doubts and fears resided in those that did break from conformism. This in turn brought about the realisation that everyone is the same, everyone has their own fears, the only difference being that some hold the courage to face them.

Alternating the basket from one hand to the other its seemingly growing weight meant she neared her home. Within minutes she had reached her doorstep only for the front door to swiftly open, the stern looks her father held ushering her to enter in haste.

Aware of his annoyance she listened to his words of shunning her joyful emotions in public, the ones he had watched her carry from their home's front window.

Head bowed she adhered to his words until gazing up to him with a giggle as she nodded and pulled gentle on his white beard.

This too gave reason for the old man to laugh, his attention now turning to the surprises her laden basket contained within.

Over lunch in the shade of their garden's sugar maple trees he looked to the seaweeds brought to him that day by his daughter's hand. Studying each piece he instinctively knew which slimy strip would provide the healing properties for which particular ailment, a skill he was thankful his daughter had inherited from him.

With each precious item of the mornings find put out in the sun to dry in preparation to be crushed into the finest of powders, father and daughter were ready to open the doors of their humble surgery in the confines of their home.

Those of pain passed through their doors as the afternoon progressed, each leaving with a concoction of powders wrapped in small pieces of folded paper of which to take in remedy.

Strict instructions were given of what was to be taken and of how much to be diluted in fresh water, an education needed for those who had often taken all at once, so producing the stomach aches which instigated a return visit.

At times ointments made from vegetable oils mixed with natural remedies of various surrounding plant life was applied with skill under a father's watchful eye, his frowns at times revisiting his daughter in her artistic sensibilities of making patterns in balm on patient's wounds.

It was not until the last of the patients entered in the closing daylight hours that talk of others turned to the taboo happenings of the village a short ride away from the more affluent Salem Town harbour side homes.

During the day no-one had dared speak of what played out in every member of their small communities mind with so many patients within the surgery. Now, as only a few remained ready to be treated the first utterances came to what had passed a month earlier.

Whispers soon evolved into full speech as those present had routinely eyed those still seated around them, at last satisfied their thoughts could be announced.

Looking to her father as both listened to those awaiting their services, his eyes narrowed to her, confirming his wants for her to not partake in the conversation, just to hear and take note of what was being said.

Taking pride in her actions of showing no intrigue into the events she now listened to she continued to treat the wound before her. She knew the details of what had happened already, everybody did, but still she listened intently in hope of making new discoveries to the growing hysteria of witchcraft.

Her heart had gone out to the victim of such callous actions, her young mind not understanding how no-one had gone to the aid of the women, her death sanctioned by the courts for reasons of not wearing the desired colour or cut of clothes supposed normal attire for those of Essex County.

Questioning such an atrocity she had empathised with her father on his lack of comprehension also, seeing his pain on not being able to guide his daughter to a true answer.

Theories as to what had prompted the hanging of a young woman came after the gruesome descriptions of the scene.

One idea was the unusual hot weather had affected the wheat eaten by the girls who had pointed the finger at the innocent whilst in raptures of mania, proclaiming acts of witchery were present, in that it was not of God's wanting for someone to dress in such a way so different to their own.

Another assumed reason came in the disputes of land and distribution of wealth between the poorer quarters of Salem Village and its more profitable neighbouring town, surfacing as a wrath of jealousy from those within the village's court system.

Taking in all notions she glanced to her father, aware his thoughts matched hers in understanding that the want of control of others had fuelled the fires of distrust, with contempt shown for those who trod their own way through life.

Talk of suspicion and worry continued until the last of the day's patients had left, leaving father and daughter to clear up from a full afternoon and early evening surgery, both aware of the reasons for their silence.

Fear and uncertainty had found its way into their home, a place that had always been one of laughter and joy, even during the recent smallpox epidemic that had taken the mother of the household from them.

In time both began to speak their views of the elders' actions of Salem Village, their concerns raised by the potions and lotions on shelf and table beside them.

It would be a further two weeks from that day of escalating accusations and chatter before their worries visited upon them.

The lunch they shared that day had been filled with laughter each had always enjoyed together. Talk of new ideas of expansion to bigger premises ignited the ambitions of the one who knew she would continue the work done now and for the rest of her days.

In knowledge of his daughter's vocation her father attempted to hide his delight, yet as was always the case she saw through his concealed emotions and gave his beard a familiar pull.

Their smiles subsided and they sat in the comfort of one another without a word until mid-afternoon shadows escaped them. Feeling sunbeams touch of skin, both retired to their surgery to wait for their first patient to arrive.

Preparing a table full of medicines needed the essence of laughter shared still lingered on, bringing forth security and joy amid times of oppression and suspicion.

The sound of footsteps outside their door brought them to switch into their guise of healers. This was soon lost in the surprise of the men who charged into their home.

Within seconds both were hoisted out into blazing sunlight, a crowd of Salem Village's community watching the abduction of the two believed heretics by the forces they had instructed, an enjoyment in their stares.

Bundled into an awaiting carriage father and daughter looked to one another. Both understood the reasons towards their capture.

As their ride made for Salem's village courts each looked back onto their home, watching in sorrow as prized powders and lotions of their profession were carried out into the street within the very wicker basket that had once brought those items there.

Staring back at each other they also understood the implications surrounding their predicament. Even though those who sat with them on the carriage's rattling journey away from Salem Town's harbour did not say a word. The gazes falling on the two captives spoke enough of their thoughts.

She watched in silence as her father spoke out in calm tones, asking the two who had accosted them if their time would have been better spent guarding settlers from the attacks of those who were indigenous to these lands. Neither of the men replied as she saw the reasoning behind her father's questions as he continued. Asking if they thought it was right to snatch an old man and his young daughter on the orders of others she realised his words vied for confirmation of their unexpected journey to Salem Village.

Recognising the men she too spoke out. Her father held silent pleasure in her words as she inquired if the one man's wound she had dressed one month earlier had healed. The intended question reached its goal and her target looked to the floor. Shame also spread over his partners features to her question of his mother's health, he too aware of the good the ones they had been instructed to seize had done for the community in ways of healing.

Both men looked to each other, a questioning of thoughts in their glances to the father and daughter. Doubts towards their commands began to take hold. Another stare to one other confirmed their reservations. A nod from one came in signal to the absurdity of the situation, but before they could act the carriage came to an undignified stop outside the chambers of Salem Village's court.

The men looked to one another again as they shepherded their detainees from the carriage and to where a jury awaited their arrival.

Hope still shone in the turning of decisions made, with both father and daughter seeing this in the eyes of their escorts.

Gathering crowds soon put paid to any optimism of reprieve, their shouts and calls overpowering the men whose courage was not strong enough to leave the comfort of acceptance and prevailing convention.

Calls of the ignorant dimmed as father and daughter walked side by side into a courtroom of dour expressions, flanked on either side by the men who would always hold shame towards their cowardly traits of non-action that day.

Fingers pointed out from those who had crammed in at the back of the room, squeezed together in the safety of one another. Shouts for demands of justice were soon quelled by the leader of the five jury men.

The youngest of the five elders looked to father and daughter stood before them, an undeniable want for power in his gaze. He stared at the remaining mumbles of whinnying crowd, bringing order to those who most literally followed the leader.

An overindulgent speech followed, the nods of his compatriots beside him prompting the absurdity of his words.

Listening to resounding insincerities of the safety of community father looked to daughter trying to find a ray of light in amongst the foolishness of others. He saw she had drifted in her thoughts.

Her plotting came, fuelled by the powerful memory of which she was blessed. Studying each face present she placed ailments next to features and a list of treatments formed in her mind. Waiting for the accusations of witchcraft now put upon them to be settled in the rhetoric of idiocy she soon began her defence.

Reeling off malady and ache that had brought each of the five elders to her and her father's door, she then began to add dates and treatments administered.

Confronted with silence she paused before turning to the crowds behind her, giving several of its members an account of the healing she and her father had given them also.

A flush of crimson cheek filled the room, no more so than the one who had unleashed a speech of lies.

Was it now she wondered, after all present had been healed by she or her father's hand, that sense would prevail.

Trying to escape the blushing features of so many the chief juror spoke once more. All looked to the door behind the elders in his announcement of a witness.

As did her father, she knew straight away that talk of her remembered treatments mattered little now to who had walked into the room and stood beside the elders and a table laden with precious medical remedies of lotions and powders to be used as evidence.

There was always one she thought on looking to the new arrival's scowl.

Recalling the day she had arrived at the surgery, both accused also remembered the melee she had caused the next day on her return.

Listening to the woman's account of the stomach pains she had endured that same night of being given treatment, daughter left father's side and made for the display of powder on the table next to the woman and grabbed a sachet of fine crushed seaweed with a scowl to the arrogance of a follower. Returning to her father's side she held the folded paper up for all to see.

Unfolding one corner she let a small quantity fall to the floor, explaining that this was the correct amount as guided by her to be taken in a single dose twice a day.

Once she knew she had the room's full attention she opened the whole package and watched with everyone else present as the remainder of the powder cascaded onto the floor.

With a pause she looked to the woman and then spoke her words to tell all that it was little wonder her accuser had suffered that night.

This caused two gasps to fill the chambers. The first was for the doubts now experienced towards such witchery charges, the second was in the woman being called a greedy pig for taking the whole intended medicine in one go.

Her father tried to supress his smiles to his daughter's description of the red faced wrathful woman stood before them, unaware his actions were being noted.

Mumbles were dismissed into silence once more as the chief elder spoke again, his finger pointed at the two accused.

His deliberation was greeted with the nods of his fellow elders and a similar agreement of verdict circled through the chambers in hushed whispers.

Father looked to daughter. He steadied himself on hearing of his exoneration and what fate his daughter was to confront, the same another young woman of Essex County had met with only six weeks earlier for the crime of not wearing the same clothing as everyone else. This time it was he spoke to the elders and all those present.

Addressing both those of the jury and the crowds in the chambers his voice took on a new form, his speech commanding strength, a miracle considering the knowledge that had been bestowed to him of the death sentence his loved one now faced.

He began with the narration towards the room of why those present and their forefathers had arrived on the shores of a new land. Talking of the opportunities provided that would not have been available in their own heartlands of Germany, Ireland, the Netherlands and the rest of Europe.

He paused before continuing, reassuring the crowd his power in oration was more than that of those who now acted as jurors, their shroud of mistrust shown in sentencing his daughter to death.

So he continued, using the sense of purpose behind community and the benefits therefore in of keeping in touch with the emotions of those who may not fit into the normal constraints of society.

Not an interruption came in his speech that reached into the hearts and souls of all those of little education and so denying the concept of free will, kept from them by the Church they so blindly followed as with matters of freedom of speech, the foundations on which their new homelands were built.

Pausing for a second time he looked over to his daughter for the first time during his talk to the masses, giving her a smile of reassurance for what he was about to announce.

In her heart she knew of what her father was to say. She wished her premonitions would be proved wrong, but the knowing of things she had always had came to the fore and in her respect for him she kept her silence.

The crowd gasped once more to his statement, that it was he who was to blame for the sorcery talked of, that it was he who coerced his daughter into following in his footsteps in the acts of witchcraft.

Looking around the stunned crowd and elders he turned to his daughter, his eyes narrowing for a moment, compassion in their expression.

The chambers erupted to his admissions, yet only he and his daughter knew the truth. It had been from the heart, from a simple want of emitting kindness that they had treated so many back to health with the medicines of nature's abundance.

His daughter held her silence in the unconditional love shown to her in the chambers of Salem Village. Even when they carried her father away she made no sound, instead resolute in her stance with no tears shed, an act of defiance as to not let those around her receive satisfaction in seeing them fall. With all eyes on the young woman who it seemed had been given a reprieve, the elder who had started the proceedings stepped forward.

The turn of events had changed all his plans and in his thoughts had damaged his reputation. Looking to all he then stared at the young woman. Her lack of emotion riled him even more and so he vented his vitriol, telling all that she too remained guilty, shown in the lack of remorse and tears for the intended death sentence of the man who had raised her.

Hysteria reined over the room, pushing the elder further in his bitterness. Going on tell all of the lies she had told of over indulgence of powder the young woman kept her sights on him, her understanding to his actions reached in seeing the wrath she had instilled in her dropping of powder onto the courtroom floor.

Deciding on immediate action the two guards who had escorted her journey approached, taking one of her arms in each of theirs they led her away to the awaiting noose, their heads still bowed in shame.

Feeling the rope prickle on her neck she closed her eyes, blocking out the hessian blindfold placed over her features, a device to shield the stares of the innocent from others.

Loose at first, the rope's slackness began to tighten. It was then she felt a hand take hold of hers and watched a white light flow through her blindfold, so pure and comforting she thought she had returned to her garden at her father's side.

"Fear no more, my child," a voice spoke softly to her as the blindfold was lifted from her.

Looking into the blue eyes of the owner of her words of reassurance she shared his smile.

"Come with me," he ushered, the light growing around them in intensity.

CHAPTER SIXTEEN

No tears were shed as her hand left the book's page. She stared at George, her eyes filled not with sorrow but pride.

Leaning back in her chair her proud expression soon turned into one of anger and distaste, her tears kept at bay once more in her determination not to sully the courage held within a lifetime passed.

"How could they?" She said.

George gave no reply in his want for her to explore the reasoning behind such actions portrayed on a hot summer's day in seventeenth century America.

Writhing in her fury to injustice she managed to catch herself and so closed her eyes to find some peace from her torment.

Watching her take stock of the situation George bided his time and looked to the stars beyond tall library window panes.

The darkness of night had deepened as stories of lives lived had been uncovered. This only led to the build-up of rich display reaching its zenith now, its band of starlight ready and prepared to fade in unison with each further page turned by the soul seated in quiet contemplation beside him.

Her eyes still closed, George studied the fine delicate features of the one he had subtly escorted through time.

In the times he had taken her hand and accompanied her from one lifetime and into the between world of which they both now resided, there had always been one overriding factor present. George thought of the quality always retained in the curious stares to him as pure white light would encapsulate all around, his own joy found in the acceptance this soul housed within.

Acceptance, this was the key to her understanding, the one thing which unlocked an awareness that carried her forward in each of her progressing lifetimes. This was shown on every page turned, read and acknowledged and he never once tired in watching her discoveries, each one as fresh as any other time encountered.

He knew the lifetimes they would peruse, the one just met with would cause a great stir of emotion. Glancing to her returning tranquillity at his side, he knew she would see through the reasons for her mounting ire. That she would find the compassion within her heart to display the forgiveness with understanding needed.

George waited for her to come to him, for her consciousness to return, renewed and ready to confront the past. With each chapter completed her tenacity had shone through her perceptions of what had been, bringing her each and every time to conclusions of great awareness, advancing her spirit to new heights of realisation once considered beyond reach.

These thoughts gave George the impetus to continue showing her the world as it had been as well as towards her eventual discovery of what was to come.

No qualms came to him on leading her onwards to fresh realisations, those that would aid her in lifetimes as yet unrecorded between the leather bound covers now shared with him.

Stirring beside him she opened her eyes and looked from the book to George and then to the star's parade above them.

With new found peace nestling within her heart she continued her gaze, aware of George's accompaniment to the cosmic display.

She wanted to speak, to tell him of the harmony her mind now held in agreement with her soul. So many times before had she been torn between the two, the want to follow just one heartfelt direction proving futile as confused views settled over her.

At George's side, sat within the vast library of books, staring up to a line of star systems she could recall looking to also in her other incarnations, she at last found the elusive serenity always desired.

Raising her hand she trailed a fingertip across the gentle zigzag of faraway suns, the familiarity in her actions mirroring the knowledge now held on the life stories already played out.

She remained fixated with what the night sky revealed in the dawning of her own awareness. Another trail of eager fingertips ran over sparkling pinpoints of light once more and she revelled in its simple delight before lowering her arm and nodding to George, aware he knew she was ready to continue.

"Healing again," she said to him.

"Another lifetime spent in the duty of other's health. But you were not alone."

She smiled to his declaration. It felt good to have read of a life where the helping of others had been tantamount to her journey. There was another aspect to her joy, even though both of their souls had come to an unfortunate end.

Revisiting the calm felt only moments before she recalled the lunchtimes spent at his side, much the way the two had done so centuries earlier overlooking a cityscape of renaissance Florence. Those treasured meals now merged with ones taken in the far eastern territories of Japan, when she too would laugh and rest easy within the company of reciprocated unconditional love.

"Your sacrifice of another lifetime was repaid," George said.

Uneasiness grasped at her heart in recalling the damp dungeons of Madrid. Revisiting such times brought forward her dislike for the injustice given to ones who had also healed the sick. It was in these vivid memories that she began to see the similarities between that lifetime of inquisition and the one set in on the north eastern coastlines of America. There was although one aspect of the two stories that bothered her.

"They were not there," she said to George.

"Who?"

"The one with green eyes, he wasn't in America but he was in Spain."

"This is true," George agreed with her.

"And neither was the one who always shows me kindness, he was in America but not Spain."

"Was he not?" George arched his eyebrows to her.

Taken back by his question, she searched within for where that soul could be. No matter how hard she tried to find him in her recollections his presence remained a mystery.

"Maybe his soul took on a much different disposition towards yours," George instigated her curiosity once again.

Wanting to remain within the American tale just experienced she understood her answers to that lifetime would be found in one previous and placed her mind back into the danger of Madrid's cobbled streets.

Searching between the lines of what had been experienced, her soul trailed through the shadows of the city's back lanes and alleyways, past markets and peoples of the capital until coming to rest before the tavern doors, the ones that had led her and her love to the unsavoury destiny awaiting them both.

"Push through those doors," George urged her onwards, his view as clear as her very own mind's eye.

Doing as instructed she walked into the tavern once again. Side stepping the moments alone at the bar she came face to face with the portly man who had promised so much yet had kept his betrayal hidden until the very last moment.

She opened her eyes revealing a shard of shock in her stares towards George.

"It was him?" She questioned. "How could it be?"

George nodded to her in his usual manner.

"Had you met before those moments in that Madrid tavern?" He asked her.

Her thoughts ran through the lives led before her arrival onto Spanish soil, trying to recall the presence of the one of white beard and kindness.

"No," she replied. "I still can't believe it is the same soul who has brought me such love. A soul that has given me so much without mention of any wants in return."

"Each soul has his entrance onto the stage of another soul's journey," George began. "And so this one's first act was that of betrayer. But can you see past his callous act?"

"He has been so kind to me since leaving that lifetime," she said. "He even gave his life for me. He sacrificed his whole being for me to live onwards."

Her words were tinged with sadness, for she recognised how even in his martyrdom his last wants had been ignored leading to her own soul's ensuing conclusion at the hands of a hangman's noose.

"And why do such a thing? Why show such kindness and ultimate sacrifice?" George pressed.

"Was it repayment of my own sacrifice in that dungeon at the hands of the Church?"

"This is precisely what it was," George confirmed. "Your selflessness did not go unheeded when letting yourself be blamed instead of your loved one."

"Is that why he took responsibility for the accusations against me in Salem Town?"

"In a roundabout way, yes, but there was another reason."

Her answer for George came in little time, growing awareness vaulting her mind forwards to the results she craved.

"His soul was repaying the harm and damage done to me."

"Yes, as must all souls who at times cause pain and distress upon others met with on their journeys from lifetime to lifetime."

Savouring George's explanations, her heart warmed to the reasoning behind another's once callous actions towards her. The compassion she had experienced before returned. The soul that had once betrayed great trust given and had ignored such a gift in greed for the spoils of treachery had shown redemption towards her in ways of kindness.

"Now you see," George sensed her forgiveness start to form.

Leaning back in his chair he watched as she churned new thoughts over, her awareness towards the actions of others. He waited for new realisations to come to her and added measure to the ideas they explored together now. That insight soon came.

"Could I have been..?"

"Could you have been what?" George asked in question to her faltering words, her mind still deep in thought.

"Could I have been equally as heartless to the soul who betrayed me at some point? In another lifetime?"

George knew his ways of subtlety were needed and he smiled to her.

"Maybe so, of these moments a soul sometimes remains unaware until many lifetimes later. Only then do answers to the elaborate and at times complex bonds shared with others come to light."

Trying to find if, how and where she may have caused pain to the soul who now showed great kindness, her recollections trekked over all that had been read in her book of lifetimes, her lifetimes. Her memories hovered over the shield she had looked to in the New York gallery only to discover its flamboyant French display of feather belonged to her hand.

"I may have met with the same soul on my battles across North Africa," she said, such recollections remaining true but out of grasp.

"Maybe," George said, "and maybe it was on the beaches of England when another battle ensued. I cannot say of such things, for all is only revealed when it is meant to be, not a moment sooner or later."

"Then I may never know?"

"Oh, you will know, but as I said, only when you are supposed to. Only then can the true dynamics you hold with each soul encountered be understood and adhered towards."

Unsure as to be content or perplexed by George's answers, she knew her only way to be now was to accept his words, accept that one day she would come to understand the factors which brought her together with those of her past, present and unknown futures ahead.

As her time next to George had advanced she had fleetingly considered the lives yet to be experienced, that was of course if there were to be any future times for her to meet with.

Aware as ever that George recognised her thoughts she had no intention of broaching the subject, her heart instead set on learning more of her past. There did however remain some trepidation of the unknown future she would soon face, of that it was certain, but for now she decided on just enjoying what continued to be uncovered in the glowing book laid out before her.

"So," she smiled to George, her internal discussions resolved. "Where will I be next?" She questioned, her curiosity exceeding her as she turned another page and onto a new chapter.

CHAPTER SEVENTEEN

The Strait of Gibraltar
7 Nautical Miles NE
Port of Tangier, Morocco
1805AD

Listening to a familiar melodic creak of wooden beam echo through the cabin, its companions of sway and tilt revealed a life at sea.

From his bunk he looked to the assortment of medicines, scalpels and bandages set out an hour earlier, preparations for ensuing battle of which he readied himself for now.

Rising from his bed he walked across his doctor's quarters and to the table in the cabin's centre. Sitting down to where he would see to forthcoming malaises he looked to what lay before him on stained teak table top.

Shrouded in amber light he sorted through the pages of written words from his own hand, placing them neat and in order before him as the ship's clock chimed once, signifying the first hour passed of a new day.

In these hours he knew his world would change. The stillness and peace found within his surgery would soon evolve into the screams and bloodletting of men caught in the battle of another's instigation. Taking in his thoughts the old doctor stared at the pages, enjoying tranquill moments before strategies of conflict began.

Word had been given of the enemy's advance. Out numbering his British fleet by eight extra galleons no fear came to him. He understood his countrymen. Each one of those aboard the thirty-two vessels surrounding his ship would show the strength needed to elude defeat.

Footsteps sounded from the decks above, falling silent as those also waiting for all to commence took rest, a solitude of mind he had witnessed many times in the advent of battle.

Returning his attention to the pages he now flicked through his fingers, he thought of the final chapter yet to be written, those final words which would see an end to three month's work.

First and foremost his work was as a doctor, a vocation as healer on His Majesty's ships, and now alone but for the company of this, his fifth book, his hearing fell back to the constant rasp of aged beam, adding to the underlying air of what was to come in the inevitable clash with French and Spanish fleets sailing westward across night's darkened wave and surf.

Putting aside thoughts of what was to come he read portions of what had been written in the month preceding. Joy evolving in the knowledge that soon what often seemed a chore was coming to a close.

It was true that he loved to write, but as with all scribes, it was on occasion a relentless task, one that would not leave its author be until all was completed.

The drive to describe and story tell pushed him onwards in his words, and so, with what little time was left to spare he positioned ink and pen side by side and stared down to a blank sheet waiting to be filled.

The churning of the past had been his focus for several months. Questioning the reasoning behind revisiting of that which had been, he put it down to the approaching finality of his own years. Closing in on seventy-one years of age, fifty of which had been spent on the seas and oceans of the world, his medical background that had mirrored those five decades guided him to write of all encountered, a treasured journey from the impetuousness of youth until now, a young mind cocooned in the elderly body of ship's doctor.

Leaning back in his chair his urge to complete his story faded. He knew the final chapter and that it could wait a little while longer.

Moments of past events pulled on his heart, reuniting him with what had already been written, his life story, his opus of the human condition.

The cabin shuddered. The muted roar of heavy chain plummeting into the depths was soon accompanied by the dull bump of anchor on undiscovered sands. With a slight list the ship settled, as did the footfalls above of those who had seen to their temporary stop. Less than three hours remained until the proposed four am assault, confirmed by cabin clock and its insistent tick towards the unknown.

Leafing through the first chapters giving insight into his younger days, memories of times spent in the medical schools of London were presented to him and his abilities in the field which were soon recognised by his peers. It would be this acknowledgement of skills that prompted his release from tutorials held in darkened chambers.

In his twenty-first year he had become a revelation and a surprise to those who taught the young in ways of healing, his natural abilities and knowledge of medicine portraying to others an adeptness never witnessed before. This played party to his removal from teaching halls and seminars and the introduction to the navy life that would see him through his years.

It would be during the first signs of English summer which saw to his first arrival aboard one of many vessels that would carry his soul over the world's watery domains.

Aside allied fleets from Portugal and the Germanic states he had set forth to the eastern shores of America before advancing across the coastlines of Europe and the palm tree lined harbour fronts of India, the like of which he had never seen before.

Steep learning curves were ridden in those early days, his skills evolving with every new dawning day as he saw to the needs of his crew who had suffered under the opposing French and Russian enemy.

By the end of seven years of warfare and at the age of twenty-eight, his training was more than complete and his life path was set out before him as treaties were signed by conflicting forces.

Superiors continued to recognise his proficiency in the ways of new found medicinal practices both aboard ship and in the clinics he would work within on his return to England's capital, a respite after years at sea. Those intervals on dry land would be hampered by a want to return to the oceans that had always held him in such fascination for as long as he could recall.

Conscious of the esteem given by others towards his talents in medicine there was another factor which gave him such reverence, a secret never mentioned but often found when in the midst of battle.

Each wound of malady encountered drew on his soul. Awareness emerged within him on every occasion when looking down to gaping wound or broken bone, producing a silent knowing of what was required to cure, what was necessary to heal the individual brought to him.

From where this inner knowledge came he had questioned many times until finally arriving to the realisation that it was simply just there and so best to just utilize this unworldly knowledge in the treatment of the injured and sick.

The ship's gentle sway gave comfort to memories of long ago. Thinking of those times he raised a smile for the vitality surrounding him during those heady days at sea. The camaraderie of the crew that was evidently there and had been present on all his travels had continued throughout his years, although there would be one aspect which was always connected with these friendships of others.

Being of officer standing there was always an unseen barrier between those of private class and although he had great company in the ones of similar authority as himself, he had always enjoyed the frequent banter and laughter of ordinary men.

This placed him an uncomfortable position, one of which would continue through his career. He had to adhere to the class system so endemic in British society, a prevalence resulting in the backing away from the playful repartee he so enjoyed below decks. This stepping back from where he felt he belonged most was of course noted by the men he was called upon to treat during conflict's hand, but both understanding and respect came from those he had absconded from. They too understood the pressures of caste. No animosity came in his withdrawal, only a deepening respect for the one who was always there for them, added with the knowledge that their doctor would treat each man no different be they king or pauper.

There had been another dynamic to the life portrayed in the pages before him. One that had seen to the many lands viewed and experienced. A compulsion of spirit had driven him to travel. An itch of such magnitude only constant movement could satisfy. This want for the new hounded his being when working in the surgeries found on the cobbled streets of his country's capital. Seeing the enjoyment of a life spent landlocked in their homelands, surrounded by the consistency of friends and family, a tinge of sadness would visit his heart, yet that pull towards new vistas only found on foreign lands would outweigh any sorrow produced in a sometime want of always seeing the same familiar faces of the known and loved.

He had of course retained those friendships, but they were resigned to sporadic moments, although all were always embraced and enjoyed in the brief visits he would observe over the years.

Thinking of those loved ones whose lives he watched grow between gaps of sometimes years on end, he returned to his pages recounting his life in hope of finding answers to his soul's want of exploration.

The year of 1768 offered great opportunities in the spheres of voyage and discovery. Talk of the doctor who spent years at sea became widespread amid the chattering's of London's higher classes, and so whenever his footsteps fell onto English soil once more the demand for his abilities in medicine were overreaching.

Such fame brought prospects also, of which were grasped when offered a place aboard HMS Endeavour.

Taking the role as ship's doctor, it was of some relief when told that no conflict would be sailed into. This was to purely be an expedition, a journey into the uncharted waters of the Pacific.

Seen as a scientific mission, both botanists and scientists had arrived at port on the day of departure. Their vocation in life was soon to be reached and the doctor on board was greeted with smiles, he now being their focal point to eradicate all fears within those never to have travelled across fathomless depths before.

This suited him fine, knowing the three years ahead of him would mainly consist of remedies for sickness from swelling waves playing on those of once sturdy, motionless standings. So too would his talents come forth in the administration for coral cuts and the briefest of wounds.

With his journey underway he would watch London's astronomers gaze into the night skies. He would leave their stares as they talked of Venus' transit over the shores of Tahiti and instead look to the heavens himself.

Each time the sights above astounded him. No matter how many times he had witnessed the scene, nor from which corner of the globe, the milky white stream dissecting the night sky into two with its collection of multi-coloured stars wrapped within always held him in awe, a joy he supposed he had forever experienced, a delight coupled with the same emotions he had towards his already known awareness of the healing properties within his soul.

This identification of his past outreached that of the years spent at sea and of those on land in his formative years. Fleeting perceptions of other lives led would visit his heart from time to time only to dissolve in moments as he tried to grasp such concepts.

Continuing across the South Pacific and onwards to chart the eastern coastlines of Australia, his premonitions of menial treatments were met with and he simply enjoyed his time amongst London's finest academic minds.

Many a night was spent listening to keen voices as they displayed all types of flora and fauna after dinner at the captain's table, laughter accompanying such times, often to the escape of monstrous insects unfamiliar to British lands.

Those nights would at times end with just doctor and his captain. Night's filled with conversations of the theoretical and theological, ones that accentuated the white bristles of his captain's seafaring cut beard. It was here that he identified his position on ship, for although he still met Endeavour's crew with some banter, he knew his place was amongst those of similar rankings. This he saw within his captain too and did not envy the loneliness that would come with such a position, for the captain would have to keep some distance from not only lowly deck hands but those of officers also. Although this commanded the respect gained through these actions, none so more than he himself and he was saddened on hearing of his captain's death by the hand of Hawaiian warriors four years following the end of their voyage together.

In the April of his fortieth year, news came of the skirmishes between British redcoats and local militia of Lexington, Massachusetts. Having spent time on the shores of America it seemed only fitting for him to be positioned as chief doctor aboard the fleet sent to quell any disputes and wants of independence.

Taking stock of a life returned to conflict he accepted his commission and saw to the treatment of those ferried back and to across the Atlantic. Many were lost on both journeys. Unforgiving seas would prove an end to the few, splintered masts and escaped metal hoists their executioner. These events would in no way be paralleled to the losses due to gunshot wounds destined never to heal. He had found some hope when the Declaration of Independence was drafted and signed fifteen months later, although no true satisfaction came to him until the formalities of war were confirmed a further seven years later in the words of the Paris Treaty.

In this treaty signed under the eyes of British history's foe, it came of no surprise that such a country intent on domination would rear its head again and again, surmounting to now on the waters in which his ship now rested, swaying gentle from side to side, cooled by North African breezes.

The clock chimed in another hour as he placed his papers back into a neat pile on the table. Taking a moment to check once again that all medicines and items needed were present he settled back, his thoughts examining what he had written.

It was not only a life at seas and all natural wonders seen that he wanted to convey, he knew there was another factor to his prose. True of course he wanted to tell of all he had witnessed, but this was not his primary aim.

Listening to the creaks surrounding him, his gaze upon manuscript and pen, he was sure he had captured the essence of his experiences. His hopes now lay that he had portrayed warfare without the romantic ideals of poets and scribes as described throughout history, that those who would read his words may discover the futility and the utter betrayal of humankind's most basic instincts of kindness and compassion.

In all his understanding over seven decades there had been one overriding element witnessed imbedded in humanity. This quality had revealed itself on all his voyages, from the settlement slums on the western coastlines of palm laden India, to the Fijian wooden huts dotted across a landscape of archipelago and beachfront besides seas of turquoise and emerald green.

In flickering candle light he remembered these places now and how on each occasion he had watched the kindness of others given to those of little. This in turn had provided him some hope towards humanity when confronted with bloodshed and the maimed.

This is what he wanted people to uncover in his words. The foundations of purity observed in others that were no different to anyone else. This revelation came to him on his travels in that no matter of colour or culture, the spirit of humankind remained relatively the same, that kindness always triumphed over atrocity.

Once again he now found himself in the world of general's games, with no thought towards the welfare of others. Of this he had seen all through his career. As his years advanced he had begun to wonder if those filled with fear and a lust for power had never been conceived, would the oceans and lands on which he had always called home have seen a drop of blood spilt in anger, or in the wrathful want of domination over the weak.

Footsteps took him from such ideals. Looking to the ceiling he put away his thoughts and once more readied himself for what was to come. The sounds of deckhands above grew in intensity. Preparing to stand he stopped as footfalls approached his desk.

No surprise came to him in seeing the lone man emerge from a darkened corner and into warm candle light.

Watching his advance the old doctor glanced to his unfinished account. Sorrow filled his heart.

"There is little need for disappointment," the man told him.

The noises of men preparing for battle reverberated through the cabin for the decks above.

"And they will be fine, feel no guilt in leaving them for you have served them and many others well."

Any sadness in not completing his life story faded in his visitor's words. He understood what was to come. Worry for those he had planned to heal diminished also, giving him a stillness of being.

As peace returned to his heart he nestled into the white light filling the cabin.

"Shall we?" The man smiled on reaching out his hand to the old doctor.

CHAPTER EIGHTEEN

Thoughts of the seas beyond the library walls that now housed her gave an added call to her heart. Almost feeling her body rise and fall across its swells she gladdened that at least one of her lifetimes had been spent on the waters always held dear.

Looking up to the windows and out onto the display that had aided her travels across the world, she saw the darkness that had given the stars great contrast was now beginning to wane. Where the blackest of density had once been now the tinges of deep blue was inviting itself across the sky, signalling the onset of dawn. Casting her eyes from the sight she wondered if daylight's arrival would bring with it the commencement of a new chapter.

"A life at sea," George said.

"Yes," she smiled.

All the sights and sounds that had accompanied her soul's journey filed her memories. Closing her eyes she breathed in all that had been, an imaginary sun beating down across her crown and cheek bones.

"A true adventure," George said as she returned to him.

"And I was a doctor again."

Her smile to the recollections of a life administrating good health onto others held another connotation.

"Yes, and you also reached a fine old age again," George joined her good humour. "Even with aging's pitfalls and slow demise."

Remembering the aches met with on walking from bunk to doctor's table her thoughts turned towards that of age as she recalled her last moments amid a Tuscan landscape, her once youthful beauty overtaken by the unyielding passing of years.

"All souls at one time think that they are the ones to do so," George said.

"The ones to do what?"

George glanced up to the decreasing night and then to her.

"That they will be the first to avoid the onslaught of time, that the lines of old age will somehow bypass their bodies and so lead them to be the first of their kind not to suffer the ravages of time's eternal fire."

It was true, she too had experienced that rush of youth where it was believed without doubt that nothing would change, that immortally had daubed its magical balm across fresh features devoid of furrowed brow and eye to temple crease.

"There is little reason to feel remorse for these effects of age upon the physical body," George continued. "And with all these insights into the lifetimes you have experienced, can you see why not?"

Delving into her heart she soon found her answers, her discovery leading to the wide eyed delight.

"We shall all be young again," she said, her excitement growing with new perceptions and understanding.

George looked to her, his pleasure equalling hers.

"Now you are glimpsing the cycle of life," he said. "Now you can see how there is little cause to bemoan the effects of old age, when holding the knowledge that another lifetime will come, bringing with it the qualities of youth to be experienced again."

"And all shall be old again," she said, her realisations coming fast in her awakening mind.

"As shall a soul return to being young again in its next incarnation. When a soul uncovers its understanding of how it will live through many lifetimes, only then may it settle into enjoying every passing year its particular lifetime experiences."

"I will be eighteen again," she whispered in her own understanding.

"As, at times, so shall you be eighty also."

Falling silent as she considered her new discoveries, which she was sure she had uncovered at George's side many times before, she looked round her to the books lining the walls around them. Aware that each one held stories with herself featured within no matter how small of large a part played her thoughts ran to the lifespans held by these authors. This led to her own wonderings of the length of years her own incarnations had held within the pages of her own book. There did seem to be a balance of years lived.

Thinking back across the centuries she concentrated on the years each of her lifetimes had taken.

The one of snowy landscape and dreams of new lands had but few years, those of which she guessed at as being no more than thirty. Recalling the old woman doctor and her trek down to the eastern shores of England, her years had proved many more, matching it seemed those of the doctor whose life had been spent at sea. Another of advanced years came to mind and her memories filled with thoughts of the former Franciscan monk of Florence, the artist's model and artist in her own right who had ended her days in the same settings on Tuscan shorelines. So too did recollections of Hiroshima's famed artist who had spent her younger years entertaining the rich and powerful of Japan.

All these had lived long lives, each reaching a well-regarded potential, but, she thought on, what of the others, what of the French knight, the healers of both Spain and America whose years had been cut short, often by the hands of those filled with fear of others lack of conformity? What of these lifetimes, when prospective successes had not been met with, potentials lost within the shortness of years?

Turning to George she saw he expected her next question.

"The lifetime I have just left in New York," she asked. "Why were my years so little, why didn't I reach the grand years I've done so before?"

"There are many reasons. These books you see around us," his arm swept across the room. "Each one contains the lifetimes of those you have met with, no matter how brief."

Following his lead she too looked over book spines of faint glow.

"Within every chapter," George continued, "your influence on events is portrayed, as are theirs within your own chapters."

"I have a part to play in their lifetimes as much as they do in mine."

"Your presence is as needed as theirs is in your own chapters, as are your actions made within the storylines and subplots that encapsulate another's soul."

"And that includes how many years I spend within another's lifetime"

Beginning to grasp the strategic allotted lifespans required for the complexities of her own and that of others connections George pushed forwards with his explanations.

"A soul seldom recognises how much influence it carries towards another encountered. At times it can take a lifetime to provide the inspiration desired, whereas sometimes just the briefest turn of word can deliver the necessary wisdom to advance a soul forward to greater understanding and compassion towards others."

"But how does this account for some lifetimes ending at such young ages?"

"It is not only a soul's words or actions that can affect others, sometimes it is the period of time that delivers the greatest teachings."

"In what way?"

"In many ways," George replied, preparing his answers. "Sometimes our early departure from one lifetime can leave those left behind reason to explore the motives and standings within their own lives. Questioning of their own mortality comes to light, bringing thoughts to them of those souls they feel closest towards and of the impermanence each holds also."

Listening to every word George spoke, new worlds of awareness began to open to her as she continued to learn of her sometimes early demise.

"Sometimes the loss of a loved one of such few years leads a soul in a different direction along their life path, where the once lacking appreciation of others comes to an end and so prompts gratitude towards all those found within their lifetime."

"And of grieving," she said, her thoughts returning to the ones she had shared her life with over many lifetimes. "In the loss of someone close, only then can we understand that loss and so become aware of the heartache we at times provide to others."

"A full circle of life," George said, "each soul giving and receiving lessons of love and loss, each emotion experienced to the highest, bringing out the resources of kindness and sometimes humility of forgiveness needed in a soul's personal development."

This time it was she who nodded. Understanding the reasoning behind her sometime briefest of lifespans, no anger towards potentials being cut short or a carrying of guilt towards leaving others through self-sacrifice remained in her heart.

"And of the one we have learned of and his voyages across the globe?" George asked.

"He too played a part in the lives of others," she said.

"Of that he did. Throughout his long years he endued the value of life, aiding those to hold as long a lifespan of years as his own, and so touching not only the ones he saved but those they knew of and not he, for the relatives of the souls rescued from an early passing continued to be influenced by the ones saved."

George began to laugh at the bemused expression beside him.

"It's so complicated," she said.

"It certainly is," George laughter faded as he looked around the library and its throng of books. "Each lifetime written of on these bookshelves contain not only your own presence but that of others who also have their own libraries that include other soul's stories you have never met with, and so on, and so on."

"Endless," she said, her view now to held on the books around her. "But how can I manage all these lifetimes?"

"It is very easy," George looked to her. "All you have to do is simply focus your compassion and kindness onto all you meet with, no matter if their reaction returned to you is good or bad. By doing this these eternal libraries, stories and chapters belonging to other souls will look after themselves, and with hope such souls shall carry out the same love and compassion towards others they meet with also."

Taking her time to consider his words she imagined all the owners of every book showing the same care and kindness to a stranger that they would towards a loved one, and although she was aware that the world did not always work this way she hoped that one day it would.

"One day," George whispered to her as both turned their attention to her own book.

"Yes," she smiled at such thoughts. "One day" she echoed his words before delving into a new chapter.

CHAPTER NINETEEN

Zurich, Switzerland
1916AD

Glaring down in the advent of dusk to wet orange and red leaves spread in chaotic pattern across cobblestone polish, she collected herself from her momentary slip and continued onwards.

Although a Zurich autumn contained its own beauty, this was now her third experience of winter's seasonal prelude which in no way matched that of her cherished Paris.

Each closing season signified her self-exile from the city of her birth, a want to return to Monmartre streets pulling on her heart in its wait for those at war to complete their games. Even though she yearned for Paris, she found some comfort in the way of life the Swiss undertook. One she too had immersed herself in.

Careful as not to slip again on the fallen leaves of the promenade now walked she looked to the gentle swells and currents of the Limmat River at her side.

She often thought the waterways dissecting her temporary home mirrored her own journey through life. Flowing effortlessly in stages as did she, there would always be the tempestuous eddies which would tempt and more often than not overpower her emotions, as so too similar maelstroms would lead on to defeat the strongest of swimmers.

She shivered in the cold weather always despised and pulled her coat collars up to ward off the river's advancing chilled breezes. Looking ahead she dismissed all analogies towards her life and present position within it. Aware such thoughts would soon escalate into the most elaborate of unknown scenarios she kept her feelings on a tight reign. Finding her footing on the pathway leading to her chosen destination she strolled onwards, still a ten minute walk away in the city's impending nightfall.

Thoughts of situations both good and bad entered her memories again, prompting control over her passions to falter for a moment. Her pace slowing, she took a deep breath in want to avoid any mind games her internal self now wanted to play.

Unfounded illusions of what may lay ahead haunted her, yet there was a remedy for this hampering of mind, a simplicity of understanding her soul carried and a knowledge she only wished she had discovered in the years before today, her thirty-fifth birthday.

It had been in front of her all along, all through the turbulent moods acted out within the amphitheatres of career and love. Some would say her emotions were expected and were the true sign of an artist, but those of such words were not the ones who had to partake in the varying emotional range experienced in a day, every day.

Most assumed her solace came when with brush in hand, canvas and paints before her. How wrong they were she would consider, knowing of the lack of peace the internal want to create the images held within them to be aired for all to see.

The satisfaction she was often asked of how it must be so fulfilling to finish another piece of art came as a foreign concept to her, but how could she explain to someone that the only gratification and pride established were in the fleeting moments when the mind shifted from the old and onto a new fresh canvased landscape of nothingness, awaiting to be touched in painted imaginations. This constant need to paint gave her the famed approach of others in their respect for her prolific output.

It had only been due to the inborn kindness she had always carried, even in times of artistic outburst, that had subdued her want to tell of the real reasoning behind the peace she at times felt.

The minimalism of her cure for tranquillity of mind enthralled her most and so had found a way into her current paintings since its discovery.

A smile to the darkening waters she now left for picturesque Zurich side streets was accompanied by thoughts of the solitary life she now led, an aloneness which brought such great contentment and had seen to the answer for her searching for harmony throughout her young adult life.

Walking between the more affluent homes of Zurich's riverside streets she smiled to the flower boxes hanging from stained window frame above. Her delight was not in the decaying leaves now present, but for the memories of summer when each wooden garden housed overflowing blooms of pinks, reds and whites.

Such vibrancy had found place in her own artworks over time spent in a foreign land so different to hers, her smile revealing a reminder to the much needed colours her canvases once produced.

This lightening of spirit in her career had transferred into her own being, bringing with it not only new clients for her paintings but a wealth of suitors also.

Continuing her path, the streets darkened around her with every footfall she considered her position amid the art crowd of neutral Switzerland. Neutral had become a defining world for her, its connotations of the bland and inspirational proved well in her present surroundings, the tranquillity of life amplifying her wants to return to bawdy Parisian quarters and the delights therefore found within. Imagining those boulevards and avenues now, her desire for the salacious increased as word spread of the emergence of Spanish artists who brought a certain zest and verve to the artisans of her city, devoid of the constructs of freewill and expression she had encountered of late.

She knew she was difficult. Others were aware of her capricious ways, yet this never hampered the friendships she held. Beneath the at times austere, unapproachable manner she conducted herself under, those who took time to get to know her truly were always endeared to the kindness of heart soon discovered. These glimpses of her soul would then be set free within the circles of those she trusted.

Another smile came in knowing how at times she would play on such awareness of her emotions by others, giving her the delight of being able to say what she wished with no fear of reprisal.

Affairs of the heart came and went, but she found that the more she delved into her work these liaisons had become less frequent.

It was not that she did not want anyone to share her solitude, an expression she took great delight within its play on words, it was just that those with the strength of character needed to keep up with her ways were sparse.

Compromise had been a quality learnt only in previous years and those of romantic pursuit faltered in the denial of a woman of strength seldom encountered on the battlefields of love. This had been the attraction held towards her and not only her renowned unique beauty. A want of conquer amongst men, a want of conquest over a self-assured mind. A challenge so many had failed to reach.

The full darkness of night had formed while consumed by her cross-examination of relationship's grounds. Near to her destination her pace slowed allowing more time to examine her solitary stance in the affections of another.

The want for companionship had waned in the past seasons. Springtime had seen to its beginnings and she now recalled the fateful meeting on the banks of Zurich's waters.

Looking up to the emerging stars of cold Swiss sky, her heart remembered the words spoken from the lips of aged Spanish gypsy sat on

Lake Zurich's northern lapping waterfront.

A deep Spanish accent with hoarseness of tone had told of the luck received now and in future times concerning career and home. These wants of knowledge had ticked each box but for matters of love.

Taking the courage to ask her reply came in a wry smile. Once more the gypsy examined the fine lines her hand portrayed. Another smile came and words were spoken on the subject.

It was these words she revisited now. Yes, it was true that lovers had come and gone, yet it was being told that these and all to come were right for her, leaving the only reasoning being that it would be up to her to decided which one to give her heart to and so remain at their side.

Familiar calls broke her from the premonitions of Romanic origins. Reaching her journey's end she waved to the group, her friends of performance artists, poets and painters. Warmed in the closeness of their presence she approached all, ready to walk through nightclub doors and to see others enjoy her exhibition across its walls of canvases large and small depicting images defined by the nocturnal unconscious dreams of herself and others.

Pigalle
Paris, France
1925AD

Grey skies parted to offer slight relief to those beneath Parisian autumnal rains. Walking steadily with purpose in her stride she left the café behind, fuelled by the pastis warming throat and chest. Any rush held faded, her morning tipple providing an ease to her pace.

It had been many years since she had posed for another artist. Her days spent in Zurich amid exiled bohemians such as she seemed a lifetime ago, a time so different to the moments she passed through here. Nights she thought would never end, where drink and inhibitions ran free in hidden cellars below Monmartre streets or in Pigalle's more insalubrious secluded backrooms. This gave her the spice of life needed to accompany her vocation of hours spent alone with canvas and brush.

Waltzing between pedestrians on her route east across the city, recollections of Zurich's moments gave respite to a speeding mind, a calmness of being remembered on the Limmat River's peaceful promenades when trying to find some peace from the constant bombardment of new ideas and compositions crying out to her soul for attention, a trait which although at times bothersome kept her ahead of Europe's continual changing movements in the fields of art.

With the rains kept at bay she walked onwards, eventually coming to a halt at the base of the stone steps that would lead her to the artist she would sit for that day. She stared over its many stairs. It was not so much the steepness that caused her avoidance of the short cut that would see to an early arrival. There were two other influences taken into consideration.

Looking to wet orange and yellowing leaves scattered across each step, memories of misplaced footsteps on Zurich's streets and the ensuing slips that often followed came to her. Not prepared to take the risk she left them behind and continued eastwards, her heart enticed by the sight she took great joy in ahead, the second reason for her evasion of hazardous climb.

That view which gave such joy soon arrived. Standing at the base of a criss cross of steps leading to her delight she peered up to the white stone basilica perched atop Montmartre's cathedral, a sight which always brought her pleasure.

She never understood how the architectural forms made by those who used their chosen religion to control the lives of others gave her such enchantment, it just always had done. A happiness found in her youth when traveling through Italy to discover the painting styles of long passed masters.

It came of great surprise that instead of finding charm in the genius of centuries old brush strokes, such allure was found in the façades and porticoes of holy grounds, with the cathedrals of Florence taking precedence over compositions of the biblical and mythological.

As she had done so then within Italian sunlight, she watched Paris morning sunbeams play over raindrop shine, the Sacre Coeur's copper and lead beading muted in amber light.

A smile to those remembered Italian days came to her. These memories of foreign lands stimulated other destinations. One place in particular called on her again that morning, a recollection she visited more often than she would admit.

Near on a decade had passed since that day. Still it would play on her heart. Those gypsy words had seen to some truth over the ten years with both work and her career paths proving correct, although she knew her success lay in hard work on her part and the grasping at opportunities when they had arrived. There was one aspect although that if went unchecked would soon fall into obsessiveness.

Now reaching her forty-forth year still no suitable suitor had arrived. The passage of time had provided many, yet once more the want to dominate seemed ingrained in them all. Thoughts of her own descriptions of being difficult were dismissed in age's relentlessness. No longer did she see herself afflicted by the problematic moniker she would parade sometimes with pride. If her title of being difficult came from her steadfast independence of spirit and freedom of speech which often challenged the male standings around her, then so be it.

It was her individuality and eccentricities which attracted them in the first place she would realise, leaving disbelief to why another was so intent on controlling the verve of another they were said to love. Was it that they did not have strength of will themselves she would question as another left her side, or was it the concluding realisation that the enchanting essence another held was not to be taken by those who did not hold such vigour and dynamism naturally?

Shaking the last raindrops from her hair she also shook away the notion of meeting anyone. Too much energy had been wasted on the foolish pursuit of companionship she decided, and had done so for days.

Taking a moment to enjoy the last morning sunrays across white marbled dome her view fell to Sacre Coeur's large wooden doorway as she climbed the stairways leading to the beginnings of Montmartre's cobblestone streets and lanes.

Thoughts towards the one she would sit for accompanied her climb. They had met many times before. Their talks at first amicable, she had warmed to his Spanish charms, although she also saw through the wants imbedded within him, leading a strict denial to his advances on each occasion. This had intrigued the emerging artist's sensibilities and he in time took to friendship with her, a realisation evolving within his soul that amity undoubtedly outlasts that of mere physical liaisons.

Agreeing to his want of model formed a bond among the two. Now that day had come where she would at last pose for him, the arrangement between them seen through the eyes of friendship by both parties. He finding new insight that every beautiful woman encountered was not necessary there to be conquered, she in her awareness that although his success and charms were attractive, there was foresight to the quagmire such an engagement would produce, portrayed in the consistent need for drama he and his fellow countrymen seemed to always desire.

Reaching the summit of her climb she turned to the Paris view she had always adored, the scene missed dearly in her time sent in Swiss exile. Lost within her surroundings a voice beside her pulled her heart back into reality.

Turning to the soft words spoken she gasped aloud to who confronted her. She raised a hand to her lips, lowering her eyes from the stranger, hopeful her reddening cheeks would soon fade.

A smile came from the one who had approached her with his want of directions. Raising her eyes to his, her cheekbones retained their crimson glow as she answered his enquiry. Aware of time's march, her want to leave grew into obsession of staying at this unknown man's side. These feelings multiplied in seeing his mysterious awareness towards her need to remain. It was then she asked her question.

Taken back by her offer of dinner, he smiled again to her forthright nature rarely met with. His agreeance brought an end to their brief meeting, and so as she watched him leave any loss of joy in longer being at his side was replaced by the prospect of eating together that evening, together.

Seeing him glance back to her from the base of her climb confirmed her thoughts, those words said years earlier on Lake Zurich's waterfront. Disappearing from her sight she turned to her beloved cathedral and then made for the sunlit studio that would see to her day of stillness.

Walking through the lanes she knew well, passing by cafes and bistros at the beginning of a day's business, each of her footsteps were accompanied by memories of the one just encountered, questioning her recognition of the stranger's green eyes and the flecks of gold which danced within them.

The day went as planned, or more so how she had expected it to go. The predictable moments of laughter and flowing wine were interspersed with manic activity of brush and frowns from her host.

The rollercoaster of temperaments prevailing in the studio overlooking wet Montmartre lanes and alleyways held no surprise, she herself prone to the artistic outbursts provided. It had been the disbelief of the two other models present to the range of emotions presented that had caused her to smile as each stood in line in various dancing poses.

Caring little about her appearance, aware what would be represented on canvas would hold no bearing to accurate feature or nuance, her gaze would fall often to the display of streaked oil paint across wooden tray acting as pallet, her view returning each time to green and gold tinges found upon the artist's trappings.

Shaken by the one met that morning, she questioned their second meeting to come that night, her internal inquiries leading to the wonder of how it felt right to have arranged their meal in haste. These thoughts kept her mind focused on stillness throughout the day and aided in dismissing the familiar eruptions of genius before her.

As the daylight hours began to fade so did the creative energy within the room. Time was called in the opening of more wine and to the calls of why she declined their offer to stay and partake, keeping an air of mystery about her in giving nothing but a grin towards her reasons.

Leaving the other to their jollity she steadied herself on stumbling for a moment on the studio's steep stairway leading to the streets below. An afternoon of wine will do that to you she told herself. Determined to dispel her unexpected light headedness a want for coffee overcame her. So much rested on her dinner tonight, of this she knew. She felt it, sensed it even.

Looking to the time she had two hours in which to return home, change and then arrive back to the arranged setting where they had first met. Calculations to that appearance came forth as she rushed though streets sprinkled with the fresh rains that had arrived to the city all day.

A near slip of heel and stone enhanced her need for strong coffee now desired. Taking the time into account, she knew in taking the shortcut avoided that morning would aid a prompt arrival to the one whose green eyed gaze had kept her heart and soul enthralled all day.

Turning onto the lane that would lead her swiftly homewards, she soon approached the lip of the steep stone stairs cascading into the streets below.

Under darkening skies autumnal winds provoked a vortex of leaves to weave its way over rain drenched granite, each step providing a level to rest on. Her hand reached out for the central banister running top to bottom along the staircase. Hesitating for a moment, decisions of turning back and walking the longer way were soon disregarded, her want for time reigning upmost importance.

She placed her hand on metal handrail cold to the touch, steadying herself once more as breezes picked up around her.

Evening clouds closed in bringing an added darkness to her surroundings and her eyes closed in the swaying movements her body now gave. Clenching the rail beneath her fingers she summoned her eyes to open. The day's second gasp came from her to what she saw, the body lying motionless halfway down the steps before her instigating her reaction.

Looking to the woman cast across the steps, head facing towards an intended destination, arm outstretched as to cushion a fall, she felt some relief on seeing a lone man walk to the victim. She frowned as he ignored the unfortunate casualty and continued his climb towards her.

Waiting for his arrival, shock coursed through her body on seeing the woman spread out below shared not only the same coat as she, but also that the rest of her clothing matched hers.

Any anxiety held within her faded on every step taken by the man's approach, her mind no longer regarding is strange that the body dressed as she remained so still as he at last stood beside her.

"And here we are," he said to her, his voice warm and filled with kindness.

Looking from him and to who lay at their feet, fresh awareness came to her, an understanding of the situation that was not without great disappointment.

"You will meet again and again," the man told her. "Your recognition of one another is strong after all these years."

His words were greeted with a nod as she reached for his hand.

"And so you begin to recognise me also," he smiled to her as white light flowed towards them over the steps she had intended to take.

CHAPTER TWENTY

A tear fell from her on leaving pages telling of a lifetime closing on the steps of Montmartre. She knew the reasons for her sadness, having identified another life where promises of anticipated encounters were not met with.

"Again?" She said.

"Again," George replayed her words aloud before looking to her. "And what of the one with green eyes?"

"The one I didn't get to meet with for a second time?"

Memories of the life she had just left came to her, the rawness of such moments tugging on her heart. Turning to George her view left her book and met with his.

"But you did meet," he said to her.

"Yes, but we were supposed to meet again that evening. In Paris and in New York."

The sorrow within her eased as she listened to her own words, a smile coming to her on observing the oddness of her declarations of having dinner with the same soul in locations separated by both distance and time, thousands of miles apart and over a hundred years in between encounters.

Understanding her new found amusement, George pressed onwards in his want for her to learn more of situations presented as night time had formed above them only to now make its slow descent into dawn. Glancing up to the lessoning blues and blacks that had accompanied their journey he turned his attention back to the one he guided.

"Tell me," he said. "On both occasions when your life came to a close before your expected second encounter with the one with green eyes, have you considered how his life continued after your passing?"

Taken aback by George's question, it dawned on her that she had in fact never reflected on how the soul she had met with across the centuries had reacted to her nonappearance.

"Well, I did have a good excuse," she said, producing desired laughter to come from both she and George.

"Yes, I suppose you did. But, would you like to know their feelings when you did not arrive to meet with them?"

Cautious to the opportunity given, she wondered if she really wanted to know the true inner feelings of the one with green eyes she had longed to meet with each lifetime. Was it wise to delve into the feelings of another regarding herself? To be confronted with the raw honesty of another's emotions concerning her own soul?

"It is up to you," George told her. "Are you not curious?" He added, concealing his smiles to already known answers.

"I think you know already," her eyes narrowed to George's mischievous questionings.

"Then where do your insights into another soul's sentiments lay?"

Needing no further push she stood and looked around the books lining her and George's table. Trying to work out where the book of lifetimes of the one she would encounter, the one with green eyes she felt whole with when at their side, she at last turned to George.

"Where else could it be?" She smiled to him and walked to where she had discovered her own book.

George watched her leave his side and continued to do so as she made for the bookshelf and stared at the space the retrieval of her own book had made. With a single glance back to him she then reached for the book next to where hers had sat. Taking it in her arms she held its warmth close to her much the way she had done so with her own and walked back to George.

Placing the book down next to hers, she took her seat once more and reached forwards. Her eyes closed for a moment as her fingertips ran across its leather cover, its appearance close to that of her own volume of lifetimes passed.

The warmth of her loved one's book brought a smile to her and she opened her eyes and looked over to George.

"Open its pages," he said to her. "Feel no trepidation, for that is why this soul's book is here, so you can see what another's perception towards your own soul is, so you can see how your actions have touched another's heart at one time or another. This is why all these books are here," his arm swept around the room again motioning to each book present.

Following his view onto the thousands of book placed around her, she leant to the one now settled before her and opened its cover to reveal the first of chapters.

Knowing of the two chapters she wanted revealed to her, curiosity got the better of her and she looked to the opening words that matched those of her own book.

Her finger traced over the same count of years that the story presented to her now showed. Shivering to such accounts, she read brief and quick of another's view of her soul leaving to find a home across frozen wastelands for them and their kin.

Looking to George she accepted his hand to comfort the emotions felt in reading of the heartache experienced by a soul mate's unrequited wait for a loved one's return.

This insight brought with it new understandings towards her own soul's actions. Although she was aware her want to find better pastures for those cared for bore only good intentions, she saw there had not really been any consideration present of how those closest to him felt about such actions.

"The courage you undertook on your quest takes on a different mantle now does it not?" George asked her.

"Yes," she whispered, her head bowing in the slight shame surrounding her now in her exhibition of holding little contemplation towards others and their feelings.

"Feel no guilt," George reassured.

"But I just left. I know I didn't want to, but I did all the same without considering I may not return."

"Yes, but you did so with good intention. This is all that really matters, all that counts. Your intentions ran true in your want to care for those you loved."

"But I didn't think of the consequences."

"Well of course not," George squeezed reassuringly across her palm and fingers. "How could you have then? You were just taking your first footsteps along a journey that was to carry your soul across a span of thousands of years."

"I still had a lot to learn."

"Precisely," George smiled. "And as you have read in your own stories of lifetimes spent, those lessons came in the forms of locations and people met with on your travels through time. Your soul showed its first merit from the commencement of your revealed incarnations."

"That my intentions were true, that all I wanted to do was help those I loved."

"Exactly," George's smile grew in her awareness. "Now," he released her hand and settled back in his seat. "Read on and discover, let the stories of another unfold before you."

Returning to the book she began to turn its pages, her eyes scanning for the familiar, locations and situations that struck a chord within her heart.

Although the book she now leafed through appeared the same thickness as her own, on examination she saw that not all the lifetimes contained corresponded to her own. Remembering her own lifetimes that had not included an encounter with the soul always recognised for their striking green eyes, regardless of sex or race, then it seemed only obvious that those lifetimes without her presence had been lived elsewhere at similar time.

A tinge of jealousy came to her in such revelations as she wondered who had loved and held that soul the way she longed to do in times of their absence.

Envy's destructive energy soon transformed into the tenacity she had always carried and so she continued onwards in her vocation to read of another's views towards her.

Continuing past a lifetime lived of differing location running parallel with her own as an eighth century doctor, she turned the pages until reaching the account of where they had shared a life, albeit only momentarily.

Focusing on the words presented she recalled her incarnation of French knight roaming over the tips of North Africa in quest of meeting with the one of green eyes whose book she read through now.

Sat aside from his charge, George watched on as the book bared all, giving insight into the thoughts and feelings of another so closely tied to her own soul. Remaining silent he admired the concentration directed onto each word and turn of phrase, her understanding coming in the final sentence of chapter read.

"She waited for him," she said to George. "She knew he would do all he could to be with her once again."

"Of that she did, yet he, you, did not arrive. Does that situation sound familiar to you?"

A blush spread over delicate cheek bone and temple as fresh realisations produced an emotional reaction within her like never before.

"I seem to do this a lot," she said, recalling the two lifetimes she most wanted to explore.

"But what emotions did you meet with?" George asked. Even though he was aware of the impeding lifetimes to which she wanted to read, he continued with his questioning of the twelfth century route towards the walls of Jerusalem. "How were her feelings to you and how did you perceive her internal belief that you strove to be together again?"

Looking to the book and then to George, she too began to understand George's intent on her pursuing all presented to her.

"She knew with all her heart that he did his utmost to find her, even in the years following his passing."

"And how did your presence influence her life story?"

Remembering the sorrow encountered in the reminder of the one with green eyes' lifetime she too experienced a similar sadness.

"The loneliness she encountered was self-imposed," she told George, "in her beliefs that I would at last arrive at her side."

"And so do you see the lesson in which you bestowed onto her?"

With head bowed her cheeks reddened once more. "Solitude," she said. "I guided her towards taking a path of solitude. So she could learn to be alone but not be lonely."

"Of that you did, but she chose another way, and so her she took a path of loneliness and craving for the soul that had been lost to her."

Aware her brief presence in the lifetime of the one she loved had prompted such sadness she reached for the book in hope of redemption. Her fingers soon trailed over a new chapter and with each page turned eliminated any residue of sorrow that may have remained from the previous encounter.

"A lifetime spent together at last," she smiled to George.

"It was, tell me of what you have learnt."

Her thoughts raced as she tried to sum up all read of, and even though she knew George already knew her words to come, she still delighted in telling him the joys met with amid words of a life lived in union and understanding.

"She knew too," she said. "She knew he was one that she waited for on that Tuscan harbour market place."

"And what decision did she make?"

The answer George's question soon came to her as she recalled her own lifetime as a former monk and his meeting with those eyes that signalled all to him.

"The same decision of mine. They both decided they would forge a new life together, living as one on those western Italian shores."

"And so they did, and so did they also influence one another's views on how to live life, brought together in the unity each desired."

Contemplating her soul and the one of which she now read of, she saw how inextricably linked they both were. This realisation gave little ease to the words she would read now, of that she was more than sure.

"It needs to be read," George gave his reassurance on sensing of what was to be revealed.

"I know," she replied in quiet tone as she viewed the heading of fifteenth century Madrid.

Once again George awaited her return and watched as she poured over every word of the Spanish chapter, eager to know the feelings towards her from the one she had sacrificed herself for.

Her study complete she turned to George in awareness of his want of answer.

"He was sad because he couldn't see me clearly," was all she said, her words enough in description of her love's want of vision towards her heartfelt sacrifice.

George knew not to push for more on seeing the effect the retelling of her story from another's perspective gave. These short words were enough for him, for he knew her awareness to the world and all that played a part within it was evolving.

Flicking through the pages of other lifetimes lived that she at last settled on the one that told of a time in Paris.

Quickly skimming over the story of an early life lived within Parisian suburbs she at last found mention of her. She smiled to his description of her beauty that autumnal morning and continued her joy on learning of his thoughts directed towards her as he waited for evening to come. Her smiles faded as she continued to read, becoming lost completely on finishing the chapter concerning early twentieth century France.

"He didn't wait long," she said to George.

"Well what did you expect?"

"Well." She paused, a slight dash of jealousy within her rising again. "He found another."

"But that is good."

"How can that be good?" She said, biting her lip.

"Think back to the words of a life of loneliness led waiting and looking out from those Jerusalem walls. Would you want your love to hold such pain again?"

Something settled within her on hearing George's question. Any envy, anger or feelings of remorse vanished from her as she came to clearly see the message portrayed to her.

"This time he chose not imposed solitude and instead found another love," she admitted, even though her admissions still carried a hint of jealousy.

"Yes, but remember those closing words you have just read of contained in another's book."

She nodded and looked to those closing sentences once more as he too many years later had become enshrouded with pure white light, and how the memories of the one of delicate cheekbone and grace had always stayed with him up until the very end of his Parisian lifetime.

On this understanding she closed the book and stood. George watched on as she walked across the library and placed the book back next to the space were her own stories would always sit.

"You don't want to know of the other lifetimes lived within the chapters of your loved one's book," he asked on her return to him.

"No," she simply replied and reached for her own book of life stories. "I know the one of green eyes had learnt the lessons needed, and that I have held some influence on another soul's progression as they have mine."

There was no mention of the encounter her former incarnation had held in front of a Parisian cathedral, nor of the one met with in a coffee shop doorway. Instead she returned to her own book, intent on reading more.

As she began to uncover another life story George looked to the dimming stars above them.

With the night continuing its steady retreat, the approach of dawn signified the growing knowledge of the one beside him, aware that when those daylight hours arrived decisions would be made towards the continuation of her own journey.

CHAPTER TWENTY ONE

Stalingrad, Russia
1942AD

After a morning searching the banks of the River Volga, he headed into the city, or more so what was left of it now.

Wrapping his oversized coat around him and pulling tight on the cord around his waist, he glanced back onto brown waters. Slight memories of happier times came to him, when he and his family would eat and laugh beside the once clear river, so different to the murky depths that had been tainted by the blood of his fellow countrymen.

Looking ahead he traipsed over mounds of broken walls now laid out in quartered brick, his eyes sharp for the prize he sought.

Each day he had visited the ruined streets of his birthplace in hope of finding the one thing which may bring back his family. Those now lost to him amid rubble and dust.

Climbing more stone hills of destroyed shop front and home he stared to his fingertips, their slight blue colour apparent in the cities approaching winter.

The first snow falls had yet to arrive, but he was aware as those of who he now shared a home with that the cold would soon come. The ones he now called family would see to his wants, of this he knew and felt great comfort in such knowledge. That new family he thought of now and would soon return to were aware of his search each day, yet not one told of its futility, allowing a ray of hope in finding his treasured item to burn within him.

With not another soul in sight he took his familiar route from the Volga key side. Walking along what had once been the city's main thoroughfare, some delight would visit him on recalling his steps but six months earlier along bustling streets, and the smiles he would often receive from the women who caught his eye in their tailored cosmopolitan attire, some even stopping to talk to him, promoting a giggle to most on seeing his blushes.

The only figures dressed in the long flowing gowns to be seen now were the charred remains of once proud shop mannequins left bald and broken, sharing the similar deathly stares he recognised in those who still lived within the city.

He fell to the ground as a distant gunshot sounded out across the cityscape. Tucked in between piles of bricks and mortar he placed his hands over his head and pulled his knees to his chest. This was where his oversized coat came in use. With a series of wriggles he soon resembled a tortoise, limbs all pulled in, its shell replaced by the dark green woollen trench coat covering every part of him.

Here he stayed for a while, enjoying his respite, nestled from the cool autumnal breezes flowing from the river, its allowance of entering the city permitted by the lack of walls which had once defended its dwellers from the cold.

Another shot rang out, its crack sounding out further away than the first. Aware he should move he remained, locked tight and secure in his own darkened world, but for the pinpoint of light entered by way of turned down coat collars.

Through his vantage point he stared past the ruins hiding him and wondered if he would ever reach his goal, if he would ever find the one thing that had once provided so much joy. He realised that in his present position that discovery would not be found. Uncurling his body he rose to his feet and continued, his shoulders stooped low in case of being spotted by those who had ventured into his city by use of force in want of conquest.

The winds around him increased. Feeling icy chills cut across cheek and brow he lowered his head, his sight still fixed on every upturned concrete slab that may reveal his quest.

He had grown accustomed to autumn's introduction to winter months and was glad of the coat handed to him in awareness of what was to come. The kindness shown to him by others who had taken him into their household was coupled by the security and love he knew he needed, and although not as significant as his own kin, the love provided was good enough.

A want to return to their side appeared as he continued onwards. He felt safe there, even in frequent night time moments when heavy artillery fire echoed around them, when they would peek out of split window panes to hot orange streaks of tracer fire flashing across derelict home and factory.

Drawing his coat closer to him he turned to the direction of those who awaited his return. It was cold and hunger had begun its slight pull upon him. Disappointment came in not continuing, but such was his mind he felt no regret. His tenacity had been admired by many, they aware as he that giving up was never an option. Deciding to continue from where he had left off he piled up a number of bricks to mark the spot and made for where he knew would see to his hunger and damaged emotions, hope riding high within him that just maybe of what he searched for may lay undiscovered on his path homewards.

The sharp corners of bricks pressed through the soles of his boots. No matter how he tried to get used to the sudden pain relief never arrived. Some let up came in the multitude of socks worn. This was not only to ward off the cold, but in order to pad out his footwear, which had also been provided by the ones who had taken him in.

A whir of machinery caused him to fall to the ground once more, pushing his body between the safety of two piles of rubble. Taking his position again beneath his coat he stared at the tank rolling across his path.

Relieved it was of his own countrymen he watched its slow tread pass by him, thinking how strange it was to see its unpainted sides and turret. He did not know the reasoning why these new war machines no longer held the conventional greens and browns, but still it intrigued him. Another soon followed. Still keeping low he watched the second one leave as well, unaware of the haste needed to make such machines meant no time was given to paint those metallic bodies.

Curled up, he felt his breaths warm his body and tucked his head into his chest. A feeling of comfort came to him again. He knew there was little safety in staying in this position, but it meant little to him. He decided he deserved this after all he had seen. Those bad thoughts came back to haunt him. This prompted him to fall into self-taught moments, and his mind recalled better times. With thoughts returning to the happy smiles of those lost from him, he pictured his family on the Volga's lapping shores once more.

The joy of a Sunday afternoon in springtime after what seemed an endless winter had been a time for them all to venture out. Keeping his hunger at bay his memories filled with the food they would share laid out on the family blanket of criss crossed colours. Almost smelling the bowls of borscht and plates of unyeasted blini, he smiled to recollections of the sharing those prized olives all adored and of course the ceremonial throwing of olive pits into the Volga's flowing currents. Lost in his thoughts he curled up tighter, his arms hugging his knees close to him. The warmth his body gave now insulated within the giant trench coat caused a lowering of eyelids and within minutes he was asleep.

A rapid volley of gunfire ahead dragged him from his slumber hours later. Disoriented by the darkness he awoke into he remained still. In seconds all came back to him and he raised his head slowly as to peek out of his coat collars.

Watching the tracer fire fly above him he looked to the moon shining down on his once city of great beauty. Annoyance came to him that he had slept, his heart wondering how his new family would perceive his absence. Tucking his head back into his makeshift shell he waited for the gunfire to die down, so used was he to the shortness of battle he now lived with each and every day.

As was predicted the gunshots soon faded, as did the screams of wounded men calling out for their mothers.

Waiting a little longer he at last decided to move. Emerging from his curl he stopped before standing and looked to the night sky. Memories of the past visited him once again as he remembered how he had shared such a sight with the ones of those springtime riverside picnics. Only now it was he alone who traced his finger across the milky trail filled with starlight cutting the night sky into two.

Enjoying the cosmic display which always brought such delight, he at last rose from his temporary nest and began his trek homewards.

As moonlight cast a silver sheen over each mound of rubble and half razed wall he looked to his shadow stretched out in diagonal slants before him.

The place that caused most heartache lay ahead. Aware there was no way around that which gave such pain he continued. Some optimism entered his heart on thinking if his search would come to an end there this time.

It had been on the very spot he approached now that the others had found him. Still in shock after his home's walls had collapsed inwards under the volley of gunfire surrounding him it had only been he who had escaped.

Thoughts of his loved one's silence following the implosion of all he had ever known hung to his soul, as did the endless questioning of how such a thing could have happened. These thoughts carried through his mind as he considered why he had been the only one to survive. These memories evolved into recalls of the ones who had pulled him to safety, taken him into their fold and provided him with a new home.

Shocked at first in his wants of continual return to his former home, his new family soon submitted to his search for the one thing that would give him peace and so each morning watched him leave their doors in hope he would at last find solace in the thing most dear to him.

Thoughts of that item washed recollections of sorrow from him, the tenacious spirit he had always shown returning as fresh hope came in the guise of the tanks he had watched roll past him. With increased footsteps he charged ahead, wondering if those unpainted tank tracks had maybe uncovered that of which he hunted for.

Dark shadows wavered from side to side as he darted forwards, faltering at times on his frequent stumbles across his neighbour's broken homes.

Ignoring the grazes and cuts displayed across his hands from each fall he slowed as his former family's home came into view.

Not knowing if it was right to raise a smile, he looked to the area he searched within for so long and to the ridged tank marks running across the eastern corners of the household where laughter and cheer once boarded.

Racing forward he came to a stop. The tank's ribbed track marks playing soft beneath his feet he stared down to what had been uncovered. With haste he went onto his knees.

With fingers cold and worn he scrambled through dust and fragmented stone, determination overlooking the sharp pains his search emitted. He froze on seeing his hunt had reached an end.

Taking a moment, he stood and looked to his prized possession lying at his feet, its presence giving the peace his heart knew would come on his reunion with what had once been lost from him.

Distant gunfire sounded again, its cracks and sporadic melody closing in on the one who now leant down and retrieved his goal.

Lifting it gently from newly exposed rubble, he dusted its smooth surface and held it close to him, tears escaping him for the first time since the loss of his loved ones whose lifeless bodies had lain covered by the debris bedside him.

Caring little now for the all the carnage and cruelty he had witnessed, the thoughts that played on his subconscious both day and night dissolved as his attention became absorbed in his link to those lost to him.

Clutching his find to his chest he looked to its gloss caused by tears now shed, each stream of salty tear highlighted in the moon's silver rays.

He did not hear the explosion, nor did he feel the resulting shock waves push his body flailing backwards in plumes of orange flame and shards of already broken homes.

As the dusts settled around him his surroundings regained their silver gleam. He glanced back to the body behind him that wore the same oversized coat as he. It seemed strange to see such a sight, yet no stranger than the warmth he now felt, abolishing the cold he had always disliked.

Turning from the body he looked to what still lay lovingly clutched to his chest and then to the lone figure walking towards him.

Releasing his grasp with one hand he waved back to the man who smiled to him on his approach.

With two hands placed back around his found treasure he watched his visitor crouch down before him so they could be at eye level.

"You found it at last," the man said to him.

A nod came in reply and he held out the red ball to show the one who knew of his search.

"Then your time here is complete," the man stood and offered his hand. "Are you ready?"

Looking over shattered window frames and jagged stone remains of where he had once shared a home with his parents and elder sisters, he nodded once more, his small hand finding a place within the one who now showed such kindness.

As pure white light surrounded them both, he stared up at the man and giggled, his eyes wide in the fascination only a six year could ever hold.

CHAPTER TWENTY TWO

Her actions slow, she leant back from the book, her eyes releasing the tears that had built up within them. Through blurred vision she left the page's glow and looked up to the stars. Their gradual decent into dawn's prelude emphasised her sadness now experienced.

Staring up to a fading stream of galaxies that had comforted the one she thought of now, she tried to imagine how she had felt huddled beneath the oversized refuge of a soldier's coat.

Wondering of the emotions that would have surrounded her former incarnation played heavy on her. Trying her hardest to find the key to uncovering the feeling a young mind had held amid the fallout and debris of war her search seemed in vain and she looked to George for guidance.

"Those emotions elude you," he said. "Why do you think that could be?"

With a shrug to his questioning her view returned to the same stars under which she had lived many lifetimes before, each one a focus for the solace at times needed on her journey across the centuries.

Recalling the story of her time on the rubble strewn streets of Stalingrad, she attempted once more to find her answers. The essence she sensed of those times came to her yet were quickly dismissed.

"Why push away what you seek?" George knew of her quandary.

"But it can't be."

"What can it not be?"

Taking a moment to fully understand the boy's emotional state she identified with now she looked to George. His blue eyes encouraged her to speak of her discovery.

"There was no anger present. Or any real sorrow either. Just tenacity and, and…" Her words left her as she realised the sentiments which no longer remained hidden from her.

"And what?"

"Curiosity," she said, a frown accompanying her findings.

"Well that is good, is it not?"

Confused by the emotions she supposed a soul should not hold when in a position of war torn community, an insight happened upon her thoughts.

"Was it a coping mechanism?" She asked.

"It could have been. But not so much on this occasion, can you see the characteristics your soul carried then as it does now and always has?"

Returning to the streets and former homes of a city left in ruins her heart scoured for the similarities George asked of her. Remembering the search that had eventually led to her demise at the hands of the enemy, a fragment of perception came forward.

"The determination, the want to find what is missing," she said.

"Yes, and what helped that drive along?"

"Curiosity," she said once again.

Watching George's nod she knew there was something else for her to find, another factor to uncover.

"What surrounded you then?" He asked of her. "What truly was the embodiment of spirit you held about you as you stumbled over brick and window frame in search for your prize?"

Edging back from her discovery she once more could not understand how such a sentiment could be found during and within the after effects of battle.

"Playfulness," she told him, "and a sense of great naivety."

George leant back in his chair, his smile summarising the happiness felt in her detection.

"There was," he said. "The playfulness and simplicity your soul once showed has always been present."

"Not to the extent as I had during a time of war."

"But remember the age you were, the short years you had experienced before I arrived to you amongst a hail of bullet and shrapnel."

It became clearer to her now. She had not taken into account that the senses she had searched for had belonged to a child's mind, inexperienced and to some extent unaware of the world around them.

"Yes," George read her thoughts. "The playfulness and innocence shown amid such barbaric conditions is prone to an incarnation so young. But they are the ones who hold the secrets their elders crave to find and are often tormented by in its absence."

"They long to have the same curiosity and lightness they once had when young themselves."

"Precisely that. Although these qualities remain within a soul and are never removed, more often or not the naivety and curiosity for life and its workings are forgotten, seen as childish entertainments, when really they are all a soul needs to enjoy the complexities and intricacies found within an individual's lifetime."

Joining his smiles, she began to understand George's words. She saw now how all the problems and setbacks a soul can meet within a lifetime would not be necessarily solved but instead somewhat eased, the outlook of what was viewed as childlike traits bringing respite towards all manner of problems and circumstances.

Allowing such emotions to course through her, she glanced to the book and then back to George.

"This lightness of being," she said. "If other souls reached within and identified that which they thought lost to them, then maybe the situations my own soul has found itself in throughout my many lives would have not been present."

"This may well could be so," George looked to her, his subtle ways promoting the further searching she as well as he knew would one day come.

Both looked up to the last embers of darkness through the windows above them and then in synchronicity to the book waiting for its next chapter to be read.

"Are you ready to continue," he asked her.

Aware of the few pages remaining she reached for her book, her understanding denying its approaching finality.

"Of that we will have to wait and see," George spoke softly to her, the comfort always found in his tones accentuated by his gentle air as she began to read.

CHAPTER TWENTY THREE

Tashilhunpo Monastery
Shigatse, Tibet
1959AD

Wrapping his blanket around him, he looked to the surrounding flames of flickering yak butter candles and then to the doorway, it's thick, heavy curtain keeping a harsh Tibetan winter at bay.

The drafty chambers and annexes of Shigatse's Tashilhunpo monastery were all he had ever known, yet still now in his forty-fourth year, he had never grown accustomed to the cold.

This trait had always brought delight to the brothers whom he had grown and studied with throughout his years, he too joining in their laughter held within gentle teasing as more candles were delivered to his chamber, extra supplies needed not only for the warmth each knew he craved but for the work he carried out within sacred walls.

Settling back onto his small stool his attention fell back to the white canvas in front of him and its fine pencil lined composition ready to be brought to life.

He had waited for this moment since the fading weeks of autumn when preparations for Tashilhunpo's latest thangka painting had begun.

Weeks of drying and the fine surface polishing with treasured conch shell had produced the stretched canvas he now sat before, it's edges pulled taut by intricate stitches across wooden frame.

The twenty-two days taken to draw out the favoured deities as instructed by his elders had carried him through his homeland's coldest season and he was ever thankful for the dawn meditational rituals needed to perform his artistry, not only essential for aiding concentration but for also providing stillness to any shiver of hand present amid freezing temperatures.

Studying the completed outlines awaiting his brush marks he checked once more that all was ready.

Sat proud in the center of the canvas, the smiling figure of a Bodhisattva stared at the monk. The figure that had attained Buddhahood through use of a compassionate mind stared at the monk, the eyes of which would in according to tradition were to be the last thing painted, so giving life to the painting and omitting kindness to all those who would stand before the piece.

Framed by sky with curled cloud formations above and tranquil seas below, each scene was brought together by a middle background of lush garden holding the joys and downfalls of the human condition, a portrayal of his faith represented by both man and beast.

Taking a brief glance to the paints at his side he stood and walked to the extra candles provided. Lighting each one in muted prayer new warmth flowed across the room increasing the brightness around him required to proceed.

Held within amber lit red walls he returned to his place. Sitting once more he looked to the delicate brushes utilised since his apprenticeship as a younger man.

Deciding on which to use first he closed his eyes and inhaled deeply. His instincts proved him well as he returned to reality and reached for the softest of brushes in his collection. A smile visited him in recalling its making when at last completing his training, the act of which was viewed as the final stage of an apprentice, and how he had methodically chosen each hair taken from between a goat's hoof before slotting every strand into the bamboo handle now at rest in his hand.

Casting aside memories of such times he looked to the blue and green hues beside him, the colours he would apply first in following the customs handed down throughout the centuries.

Fine powdered mineral gave the small bowl of water beside him the required blue tinge needed. Stirring the mixture clockwise in following with Buddhist belief of how life always continues forward with no thought of the past, the monk spoke the mantra which would accompany his artistic journey from first initial brush stroke until the last.

With a dab of brush into the desired blue consistency, he placed that first brush stroke, a swipe of deep blue from left to right across the canvas' top section, a hue that would lighten in intensity on flowing downwards towards a white cast horizon of the painting's summer skies.

Another breeze flowed across the room as a figure pushed the doorway's heavy curtain aside briefly to gain entry from the freezing conditions outside. Flickering candles went unregistered as the monk fell into trance, a state of being reached through preparation both in meditation and in prayer and so enhancing every measured daub of paint.

The new arrival's flushed cheeks betrayed the true purpose of her visit, a reddening not only from a welcomed candle flamed heat but from the thought of her orders, commands given by her superiors as to spy on what was being produced by the artistic monk she herself had come to know over the last two years.

Excited that the canvas she had watched being sketched out for three weeks had at last been touched with the colours it awaited, she stepped soft to the back of the room, where hidden in shadows she could watch the skill played out before her.

The monk knew of her presence behind him. He diverted his want to smile in knowledge of her attendance and continued with the full blue skies depicted before him, his concentration sustained until the last hints of azure touched the tips of blank shaded cloud formations.

The fascination the young woman had shown in his paintings two winters ago had relived him of any anxiety. Aware of the destructive forces he had witnessed his own brothers fall foul of nine years previous, the monk's only true fear now was of being made to stop his chosen vocation of thangka painting.

Over the next few days the monk would return to his dream like state on each occasion his brush met with canvas. All was watched over by the young woman assigned to him, her joy concealed from those of higher rank in fear she may be labelled as conspirer to aid those amid the oppression of a culture she had come to care so deeply for.

Both watcher and the watched had said little to one another in the time leading up to what was now their second winter in each other's company.

No words were deemed necessary as a silent respect had been reached in the monk and the young soldier. Admiration was given from she to him due to the insights he provided on producing the artistry she had herself longed to try, he for the quiet manner she portrayed, a revealing of great trust in times of his homeland's coercion. This trust found within his observer had come forth deep within her green eyes, the colour and golden flecks held within portraying a lineage of Siberian ancestry.

As one week passed since the commencement of painting, the soldier arrived to the monk's quarters to find the seas of the thangka's lower section had been completed.

Saying nothing to the monk who already saw her growing anticipation, her view fell to the assortment of paints lined out ready to be applied to the canvas' figures surrounding the main deity, each one composing of narrow black outlines ready to be filled.

Lighting more candles within the room the monk nodded to the seat beside him and then to the blank canvas set up next to his.

The soldier could not contain her smiles. Looking to the small collection of paint brushes and paints to the left of the fresh canvas her joy became clouded for a moment.

Knowing of the reasoning behind her presence within Tashilhunpo's walls, she once more fought her internal battle between the duty to her homelands and the knowledge that what she and her fellow countrymen had been asked to do was wrong and without morality.

Seeing this torment the monk motioned for her to take a seat beside him.

In the days that followed both painted side by side, he in trance and she ever watchful and ready for diversion in case one of her peers should happen into the room. This worry gave no restriction to the freedom she felt, brush in hand, paint touching delicately across her chosen composition.

Breaking from his own work the monk at times would guide his unofficial apprentice in ways of blending and using light and shade to form shapes on flattened surface. These moments took them through the closing winter months, yet it would be the first week of the year's third month that would be significant for the two souls who painted at one another's side.

Sitting before his thangka painting one morning, the monk studied that of which had been accomplished. Checking each completed area from sky to sea and to the lush garden scenes between them he then examined the painted limbs and torso of the Buddha whose features were yet to be painted.

Seeing all was in order and that today would mark the beginning of the final stage of painting he rested back on his stool and glanced over to the soldier's work in progress.

He had been impressed with her work from the first day she had begun to paint. Each following day had proved more successful than the next and after a week of playful brush strokes he had been enthralled by what he discovered one morning, entering his quarters to find not only already lit candles but his companion sitting before a fully sketched out canvas ready to be painted.

With no word he had sat next to her and looked to the design awaiting her brush, giving her a nod only a master could to his intern, all be it a secret one. Noting his praise they both stared at her drawing of a bluebird, the creature's wings outstretched, head raised high, each feather presented in fine chiselled lines pending to be filled with a lavish range of blues.

That had been weeks earlier and now he looked to the half-finished plumes of bluebird feathers, each one delicately portrayed in the shading techniques he had conveyed to her.

Waiting for her arrival he closed his eyes and delved into the medative world accustomed to, only to be thrust back into reality a few minutes later as the young soldier who had sat at his side for months rushed into the room.

Rising to his feet he looked into the frightened stare before him, his understanding to the situation coming within moments as the green eyes so rare amid those of deep dark brown flicked from him to the near completed thangka painting beside them.

It was then that both understood their time together had come to an end as the young soldier explained how those above her had ordered the halt to painting in the style of the culture they now repressed with wanton yearning to completely destroy.

The monk gave reassurance to the delicate features staring up at him, his heart breaking in seeing the film of tears covering such exquisite eyes.

He too looked to his unfinished painting. The months of preparation and appliance of paintwork mattered little to him compared to the canvas that stood beside his. He knew also the soldier who had become a friend would also not be able to complete the bluebird evolving beautifully across blank canvas beside his.

In silence both turned to their work and stood quiet and in contemplation of what had passed, both also aware of what action was needed in order for the safety and wellbeing of the thangka painter of Shigatse's Tashilhunpo monastery.

It had only taken a day to organise. The monk had not expected any aid to come from the one who had brought such news of another attempt to annex a culture of those who lived in peace, yet that help came in the guise of two events, the first of which he discovered hidden beneath his incomplete canvas.

Knowing of the dangers present he still visited his quarters before escaping Tashilhunpo's walls from his oppressors, a want burning within him to take the unfinished painting he had laboured so hard upon with him. Now stood before the canvas he reached down for the bundle wedged under the wooden easel he had always used.

Lifting the package to him he knew who had provided the much needed bedding and blanket now held to him and although he was overjoyed by such a gift he was also aware that this meant the canvas he longed to take with him would need to remain.

A shuffle of footsteps behind him delivered the second event. He eased into staring to the green eyes he knew so well, a single finger held to the mouth below them.

Following the soldier's lead, aware as she of the risk taken by them both now, under the cover of darkness they made for the monastery's southern gate which in turn would lead him onwards to the safety of another country.

On reaching Tashilhunpo's exit the final hurdle left before a journey of tremendous courage came in the form of goodbyes between the two.

Looking to one another they kept their customary silence. Once again not a single world was needed, the thank you held by each portrayed in the smile one gave to the other. With a final nod the monk made his escape.

Leaving his home and at one time security of Tashilhunpo, he tucked his blanket and bedding close to his side and looked to the milky stream of stars spread in a thick line above him. He knew such a sight would guide his journey to safety, much the same as had the green eyed soldier who now watched him now disappear from sight into the darkness of Tibetan nightfall.

Keeping within the haven of night time hours he made his way westwards. Guided by starlight it would be when the cosmic display faded that he would at last take a few hours refuge to sleep and rest before commencing an evening trek across his homelands.

Traveling along the township outskirts of Lhatse and Ngamring he found generosity and smiles in abundance. This outpouring of help towards his journey was appreciated more so than at any other time, as he knew of the repercussions that would befall those who aided him now if they were to be found doing so by Tibet's harrying government of another country forced upon his own.

Continuing onwards the dawn hours signalled new sights for the monk who had raced through the night. Each morning as the sun began to rise and stars fall behind a sky of ever deepening blues, he would look to the Himalaya mountain range to his left hand side, a sign that his path remained true west, denoted by the pink tinged snow and granite peaks that greeted him each morning.

Ever thankful for the blanket and bedding provided for him by his accomplice of escape, his thoughts wandered often to her safety among what he knew would be of great melee in the discovery of his disappearance.

Somehow he knew she remained safe, those green eyes of hers never once betraying the route taken by Tashilhunpo's absconder. Thinking of those eyes as his began to close on resting up for a few hours, reality faded from the monk as he nestled into the warm covers provided by the one who often filled his thoughts.

Accompanying his night-time travel he would recall the thangka painting left unfinished in his former Tashilhunpo quarters. Wandering if he would ever complete the piece his thoughts fell to the canvas that had stood beside his own, its composition of a bluebird etched into his mind.

Seeing the few feathers that were left untouched he concentrated on bringing the full bluebird to light, imagining the blank areas of starch white canvas being painted by the soldier of the green eyes he so missed being at his side.

It was these thoughts and ever increasing distant memories of a life lived within Tashilhunpo's sacred walls that pushed his soul onwards through the cold early spring reaches of south-western Tibet. Coupled with his twice daily meditation practice, he knew that with all the help given by those he met with on his homeland's barren, frost lined roads there was another factor which urged him to continue, this was revealed in the tenacity of spirit he had always held, something of which came to the fore as he trudged on besides the rising Himalayan peaks at his side.

A week soon passed in his routine of travelling by night and catching time to sleep in daylight hours. As a further two days came and went it would be on his approach to the border that would see to his salvation, when he would come to understand his reasons for self-induced exile.

Taking the unusual step of traveling through the day, the monk had ignored his own safety of being seen by the coercing regime his fellow countrymen now suffered under and strove onwards through thawing snows. He knew his journey into freedom was coming to a close and so acted accordingly in his want to reach the Indian border where he was sure his acceptance would be granted.

Standing before the shallow ravine briefly parting the mountains which had been his sole companion for close to two weeks, he peered into the distance to the path he would now take, his heart immersed in plans of immunity. A voice behind him pulled him from his thoughts.

Remaining still, no fear came within the words spoken to him now, his mother tongue dismissing any worry that his enemy had discovered his trail. Turning to the greeting given, he nodded to each of those present, a silent knowing that the group of nearing twenty searched for the same as he, for their footsteps had not alerted him of their presence and so would have also been undetectable to the ones they too fled from now.

His welcome into the fold was given within the first seconds of his recognition of those who carried the same culture and dialect as his own. Looking to each one, his view rested on the young man surrounded by others of larger physique. Not wanting to gain attention towards the one he stood with now, the thangka artist from Tashilhunpo simply nodded to the bespectacled young man, an action which initiated a friendship between them that would continue for decades to come.

And so, on the 31st March 1959, Tashilhunpo's famed artist crossed into India, his first footsteps into freedom accompanied by a small retinue of Tibetan political ministers, a handful of soldiers and several of his fellow brothers, each of which had shielded the revered one who now led the way, stepping forward onto foreign soil and forsaking his Tibetan homelands in want of retaining his people's spiritual heritage.

Santa Barbara
California, USA
1989AD

The sound of crashing waves seeped into his consciousness as the morning's meditation practice came to a close.

Looking to those seated around him, he smiled to the ones who helped him to his feet, feeling no pride that time's passing had led to his need for assistance.

Once standing there was little need for further aid, he knew as did the others of their humble monastery resting on the Pacific coastline that a lifetime spent seated before a canvas would one day undoubtedly take its toll on knees and hips.

This understanding gave an added respect to the master who taught thangka painting and so kept Tibetan traditions alive, he who had risked all to leave his country and in turn received great fortitude in joining in exile with the one all looked to now for guidance.

Walking with his brothers towards the dining hall already alive with pots and pans of rice and dhal, a young novice ran towards him.

A smile was raised in seeing the young Tibetan dwarfed by the long cylindrical tube he carried in his arms and another came in witnessing the relief when handing over the parcel to the great teacher of thangka painting.

It was not uncommon for him to receive such gifts. All Tibetan artists knew well of the monk of Tashilhunpo who had fled great persecution and after ten years of establishing an artistic enclave in the safe refuge of Dharamsala, northern India, had been relocated to America as to continue with keeping ancient traditions alive in the guise of teaching centuries old techniques.

A brief glance to where such an item had arrived from caused him to divert his want for breakfast and he made for the room that would soon become alive with those eager to produce the thangka of their lineage.

On reaching his studio the monk looked to his student's easels placed around him, each with images of the Buddha and minor deities in differing stages of development. Walking to his own easel he emptied it from a sketched out canvas, ready to accept what had been sent, his heart intrigued by the Chinese stamp across the top half of the tube given to him that morning.

Releasing the sealed cap at the end of the tube his eyes closed. He knew what was contained within in that moment and savoured the scents of insense and yak butter candles from three decades earlier. With great care he pulled the rolled canvas from its well-travelled casing. After unrolling it he placed it on his easel and looked to what had remained incomplete for so many years.

It seemed only as yesterday that he had last looked at the blue sky, midriff of garden and base of great ocean scenes. His eyes flowed over the piece he had left in haste all those years ago, its remaining blank sections crying out to be finished.

Studying the Bodhisattva's cheeks, forehead and eyes left to paint, the monk reached for already prepared paints and began what had been started amid a Tibetan winter of 1958.

Each brush stroke taken evoked precious memories of times gone, no more so than the one he had thought of often since his arrival onto Indian soil and further so when entering American frontiers. He had never returned to the land of his birth, nor had he ever discovered what had happened to the one with eyes of such beauty never encountered again in his lifetime.

Thought of the young soldier who had helped him caused him to pause from his work and he reached for the tube that had mysteriously made its way to him from forbidden lands.

Raising the packaging up for closer examination a small canvas emerged from within. In haste the monk unravelled its gentle curve, his eyes moistening on looking to the delicate rendition of a bluebird staring up at him.

Sitting alone in the room he had taught for all these years, nothing had touched him more than the small rectangular painting before him now.

Gazing from the window beside him out onto the vast Pacific waters he had dreamt of seeing since a novice within Shigatse's Tashilhunpo monastery, remembrances of all that had passed came to him, signified by the bravery shown by the soldier who had once painted at his side.

Setting the bluebird painting down beside him he knew what was needed and so continued with the thangka painting sent to him now by the owner of the eyes he could never forget.

Within the hour his work was complete and he looked to the Bodhisattva whose eyes were the last to be painted.

Listening to the hallways outside begin to fill with those ready for a day of study and prayer, the monk walked to the doorway of his teaching room and closed the outside world from him. Returning to his canvas he looked from his at last completed painting and then to the bluebird stood proud of place on the small canvas next to his.

It went against all his principles concerning the skills he had mastered throughout his years as a thangka painter, yet on this one occasion he was aware of what was needed.

Having had instructed numerous others throughout the years that the last part of painting was the main deity's eyes, and so giving existence to the work, he evaded such tradition now and reached for the blue paints that would in his eyes truly complete the painting of so many years.

Leaning forward he placed delicate brush strokes of blue paint to the top left hand section of sky and within minutes a bluebird hung in the air, its wings spread out in flight.

Leaning back he looked to the completed painting, his heart yearning once more for the one with green eyes, as it had done since his first footsteps across Tibetan plains and onwards to safety.

Now he had given her his thank you, for she had been the one to give him life, the one who had provided him with an opportunity to be all that he could be.

He smiled and looked to the bluebird in mid-flight, recalling once more the one from so long ago whose essence was now immortalised in paint.

"You have finished it at last," a voice sounded through the room.

The monk looked to the figure stood beside him now. He nodded, knowing exactly who his visitor was and what signified his presence.

"Shall we?" The man said on reaching out for the weathered hand that had spent a lifetime producing beauty.

The monk looked from the image of the bluebird his mind had treasured for over thirty years and then to the ocean he had always found such comfort in.

As his thoughts wandered from how different the view of swelling water was to that of the mountainous landscapes of his homelands, he felt warmth encircle his body as all faded from him in a haze of pure white light.

CHAPTER TWENTY FOUR

With her fingers leaving glowing pages she turned to George.

"You waited," she said to him.

Seeing the pleasure his actions from times past had brought, he nodded to her smile.

"This time, it was of the utmost importance that the painting was completed."

"Why?"

George watched her curiosity rise, her instinctual traits surging for answers.

"Why? So you may understand the deeper connections held with the one whose green eyes your heart reaches for."

His words played on her as she recalled moments encountered with the one he talked of now. Remembering how it was not in every lifetime that their souls were reunited, she could still taste the want harboured within her heart of meeting them in those lives without their presence.

"But this time it was different," she said, her thoughts through history catching up to the incarnation of Tibetan monk, his passing seeing to her arrival to the body that had housed her soul in midtown Manhattan.

"Yes, this time is was different. But tell me first, what do you think of the journeying you made whilst dressed in the burgundy robes of your then faith?"

Wanting to know of the connections talked of between the monk and his guard she submitted to George's request, more than aware her answers would come in their own time.

"I, travelled a long way," she said.

"Of that you did, in both journeys."

Understanding the connotations of George's words, her mind returned to the rapport held between the two who had painted together within the guarded walls of Tashilhunpo monastery. The tryst they held that remained unrequited and unspoken was one of deepest respect for the other. In these thoughts she recalled the aid of the monk's escape, of the travels taken across the rooftops of the world and the meeting with the one who would see to his destination of a life lived on the shores of oceans always dreamt of.

"You see," George smiled in listening to the thoughts of the one he accompanied through moments shared, "there was a covering of great distances, both of the emotional and the physical."

"Even in those times spent in the Tibetan monastery, I could never have imagined where I would end my days."

"And so this is the essence of the situation a soul can find itself in from time to time."

"We never know," she said, her awareness to George's words growing.

"No soul can know where they are heading or where their eventual destination will be. At times there can be an inclination, but the solid proof often wanted is not there, and so…"

"And so," she broke into his explanation, "a soul has to rely on its own beliefs that all is going to be ok, and that a sometimes constant need for reassurance isn't necessary."

"These are the emotional expanses a soul travels in the years spent within one lifetime, where sometimes similar large distances are covered as also the physical body across the globe."

Staring up to the fading band of stars that had acted as a much needed map towards her previous incarnation and so providing safe haven, she thought of all the twists and turns of not only the monk's life but of all those she had read of at George's side.

It seemed each one had also been on a journey, striving onwards into the unknown, towards goals that would reveal themselves only when and if ready.

"You understand," George said. "This is the one of the greatest pieces of knowledge a soul can retain. To understand that all has its natural course, that moments arise when they are supposed to happen, the thoughts, ideas and awareness of life's struggles and pleasures come to a soul when they are meant to be experienced, neither before or after and all in perfect timing."

This made such sense to her now as she sat beneath a window framing the emerging dawn light, its fading display of stars signifying her own awareness evolving out of the darkness of nocturnal hours. She too now saw how all her answers and perceptions had a vital pattern to them, displaying their information only when a soul was at last ready to perceive the treasured insights on offer.

It was only now in her true realisations of the flow and evolution of awareness that she understood that moments earlier she had not be ready to understand the link between monk and guard, one of which had held physical implications.

"Yes," George as ever new of her thoughts. "Now you can delve into the bonds between them, the links held between your soul and theirs as seen in that lifetime under endless Tibetan skies."

The sight of them sitting next to one another after months of silent standoff came to her. She saw the care her own soul had given towards what was essentially a jailer in way of providing a canvas and paints to allow a desire for creativity to be released. This act of benevolence towards the one who saw to her detention was of course repaid in the helping of escape, even though the one with the green eyes had indeed orchestrated her farewell to the one who had shown such kindness.

"Sacrifice," she spoke of the quality once more. "She sacrificed his presence at her side for his freedom."

"Yes, but there was more to it than the sacrifice of a soul's own comfort."

"Unconditional," she whispered her understanding, at last seeing how the love that had deepened and developed between the two souls over the centuries had reached new summits of empathy.

"Both souls were aware of beliefs and vows taken and so adhered to the constraints of a life lived in abstinence and virtue. What developed from there came in the advancement of one soul's love for another."

"An exploration of the emotional more than the physical aspects of love," she said to George, her own awareness growing.

"As a soul progresses through its lifetimes it comes to recognise the importance of the emotional love bonds found within souls met with over and over again."

"That although the physical sentiments remain between the two, the unconditional aspects of love and care become of greater focus," she replied, her new found knowledge expanding the lessoning boundaries of her awareness.

"Sometimes when souls meet who have shared so much together in previous lifetimes, a time is needed where all attractions are concentrated on the emotional aspects of a liaison made between them."

"And this is why I never forgot her. Never forgot the bravery shown in helping me escape and the thought of how she had kept the yet to be finished painting with her over all those years before providing its way home to me. This is why I always held a cherished place in my heart for the one with green eyes."

"And also why you choose to immortalise her memory in your final painting. This is why I waited until you completed the piece before my arrival."

Remembering the bluebird flying across a depicted blue Tibetan sky, not only from the words read but from her own presence sat before its actual canvas in New York, she now knew the answer to the puzzle that had troubled Tibetan art scholars for decades as to the bird's presence.

All this however seemed of little worth to her now. For who could she tell such findings too? This gave no trouble though as another question came to her.

"Did the one with green eyes ever get to see the completed painting?" She asked.

George looked to her, his eyes providing their guidance as he glanced over to the bookshelf containing her answer.

Taking his lead she left his side and made for the book that told of the once Chinese guard's lifetimes, her pace quickening on her quest for solutions.

Arriving at the shelf she reached once again for the volume next to the empty space where her own book resided and then raced back to be beside George again.

Seated with him once more she pushed her own book aside, opened the one retrieved and found the chapter they had shared in Shigatse's white walled monastery.

At times her finger trailed beneath the words that told of a life guarding the Buddhist monks of Tashilhunpo, the views held to such actions that carried a repulsion of orders administrated by those of command.

Reading her soul mate's inner thoughts of the revulsion experienced towards the mistreatment of others, she looked to George, his silent nod confirming that the one who had who she had sacrificed herself for in Spain's similar situation of an eradication of others still contained an abhorrence for injustice.

Continuing onwards, she read of the joy felt in sitting with the one who had guided them to the world of painting, the delights such actions had given which had led to the discovery of a skilled hand. This momentary insight into happiness succumbed to more sombre words as she read of the ensuing goodbye given to the one who had gained not only their respect but the unconditional love needed in aiding the monk of Tashilhunpo's escape.

Feeling the swirling mists of heartache reach to her from the pages she now read, she looked to George for the reassurance always given from kind blue eyes. Renewed by the smile received she carried on as the life story of a loved one unfolded before her.

Taking in the years that followed her former incarnation's escape, she learnt of the disciplinary hearing and eventual expulsion from the Chinese army, which after a period in prison had seen the one with green eyes who had sacrificed their freedom for another relocating to the eastern shores of her country.

It seemed the then small city of Hangzhou had treated her well. A tinge of jealousy resurfaced in the book's reader to the family and marriage that resulted in the forthcoming years. Yet it would be in the telling of such times that the puzzles of the fragmented lives of others developed into the solutions for the answers searched for.

As curiosity overpowered any existing envy she delved more into the story presented to her now, each page an insight and revelation into the intricacies of life and its often hidden surprises.

George watched her excited glances to him on her discoveries of the Tibetan painting that had taken several decades to be completed. Reading how when visiting a street market, one of the children of the former Chinese monastery guard had found the thangka painting rolled up on a table laden with Tibetan trinkets. Taking it to her elderly mother as a gift, what soon came was not only the identification of from whose hand the unfinished painting had come, but of the choice as to return it to be uncompleted.

Engrossed in the telling of finding the monk and his new homelands, the book told of the emotions produced in the one who had never forgotten the kindness her deemed captive had shown in what now seemed a lifetime ago.

Turning to the final page of the chapter, its reader poured over every word revealing its protagonist's closing moments, and how her love had looked to the magazine article concerning the thangka masterpiece of a recently passed Tibetan monk on the coastlines of California. Those last sentences brought a tear to its reader as she learnt of the joy the one with green eyes had held in seeing the bluebird depicted across a Tibetan summer's sky as a pure white light descended upon her.

"Your curiosity served you well," George said.

"I would like to know more," she told him, the book still in her hands.

"Then you must read on."

With a turn of a page she looked to the heading of her love's next chapter and then to George.

"Yes," he said. "It is the same birthdate within months of your own."

"Then..." her words faded as she leafed through the pages until finding the moment their souls had met in the doorway of a New York city coffee shop.

Reading of the feeling felt for her in their brief encounter, she continued to learn of the anticipation on meeting with her again.

Warmed by such sentiments a familiar heartache came in reading of the one with green eyes' time awaiting her arrival and eventual submitting that the owner of such delicate cheekbones was not to arrive for their dinner engagement.

"Like if Paris," she said to George, her disappointment evident to missing their reunion of souls.

"Yes," he motioned for her to continue reading.

After a brief pause she returned to the book. Turning to the next page she stopped, looked over to George and then back to the words appearing one after the other across blank pages.

"His story continues as we speak." George said to her.

Watching sentences form before her, she realised she could now in theory sit and follow his life in real time, her finger tracing beneath each moment experienced by the one she longed to be with.

A new insight came to her. Closing the book that had given her a view of shared lifetimes from another's perspective she reached for her own words.

Opening her book to its final chapter, she read its closing paragraph telling of the fading art gallery studio around her and then turned a page to reveal a new set of blank ones.

An understanding of the moments to come entered her and she looked to George.

"Yes," he smiled. "They are waiting to be written."

CHAPTER TWENTY FIVE

Glancing from George to her book's blank pages and then back to him, her awareness to what lay ahead began.

"I'm to write my own chapter?" She asked.

George placed his hand onto the table next to her book. With a smile he lifted his palm to reveal a pen which held a similar glow to the pages it awaited to meet.

"Of that you are," he said. "And now you have all the tools you need."

Reaching for the pen she hesitated. Remembrances of many times passed came to her as she viewed what lay on the table in front of her and George.

"Yes," he said, "we have sat together many times, right here at this very table."

"And I have written out my next lifetime? All of them?"

"You have."

George's reassurance to the enormity of the task now faced gave some calm to her worried stares.

She looked to her soul mate's book and then to George.

"But the one with green eyes, their chapter isn't all written. I was following it as it went along."

"That's because you were the observer and not the character. You were reading a story as it unfolded, yet the author knew of the outcome already having sat at a table not unlike the one we sit at now and wrote all that was to come."

"So, if another soul were to read my life story in real time then they would see words appearing as situations and moments as they played out?"

George nodded and then looked to the pages calling to be written.

"This is why we are surrounded by all these books. They are here for you, for reference as to what you are to write."

"But," her frowns gave away the questions that hounded her now. "But, if I have written all my own lifetimes before I have lived them, then why were some so... so..."

"So difficult?" George found her words.

Recalling all she had read of in the book that awaited not only her attentions but also her intentions, memories of the misdeeds of others towards her and the sometimes short years experienced came to her.

"Yes, I mean, why would I possibly put myself through such torment and pain?"

"There were good times too," George's blue eyes bore into her heart. "Were there not?"

Fresh memories came to her in George's questioning and she smiled in recalling times spent in solitude and rapture before a canvas filled with colour, as did her thoughts come to rest of being in the company of the souls that at times had accompanied her journey through the centuries. The kindness and nature of one particular soul warmed her heart and her spirit lightened in remembering the one she would share a romantic love which deepened with every life time spent together.

"You see," George said. "There has been a balance of the good and the bad, an equal amount of joyful times as has there been the not so pleasant."

"But why can't it be good all the time?"

"Where would the sense in that be?"

It was in his question that she began to gain the awareness needed to commence the writing of a new lifetime she and the many characters to be encountered would play out under her direction.

"Because there wouldn't be any distinct good times without those bad," she said.

"Yes," George continued his agreement with her. "And how could a soul possibly learn anything if this was not the case? How could a soul advance, and those other souls they touch in moments chosen by the author?"

Piecing together the guidance and direction given her soul began to acknowledge the awareness it would always reach as old discoveries mixed with new ideas and concepts.

"I can write what I want?" She asked, her anticipation towards what lay ahead beginning to burn within her.

"Anything," George replied. "But remember, the reasons behind what you are to portray in words. Remember the reasons for the spectacles of pitfalls, heartaches and disappointments you are to face, as well as the dramas behind the love, kindness and laughter that will interweave and interlace throughout your own unique story."

It was George's requests that fulfilled her final understanding. She now understood the reasoning behind situations of goodness and malevolence as fore planned by her own hand, a weighing of emotional scales as required to provide the equilibrium of her own doing.

"And of those I meet with?" She said, her thoughts remaining with the ones closest to her.

"They too have lessons to learn. And although you at times shall be the instigator of such educations, remember that they too will provide you with as many lessons you yourself must confront and master."

"But, if it is me who is writing my own story, how can I correspond and link the lifetimes of other souls who themselves have written their own exclusive stories with me playing a part also?"

George smiled again, his pleasure found in the question the soul before him would ask on each occasion they would find themselves together within the vast library of her and other soul's life stories.

"As I said before," his arm flowed across the books lining the walls around him. "All these books are here for you, to aid the threads of meetings and happenstance you are to write of, to provide the correlations at times needed in bringing one soul's lifetime in parallel with another's, or indeed with many others.

At last her awareness came as did the smile harboured deep within her. She too looked to the books around her, her understanding to their presence achieved. Once more her memories filled with moments of ages passed, of the times spent writing at the table she sat before now, of the many trips she would make across the library floor to book shelves calling out to her for her wants of cross reference and insight into the soul stories of others.

"Listen," George said on feeling her comprehension brought to the fore. "Can you hear that?"

Falling into silence the noise came slowly at first. Closing her eyes she began to make out familiar sounds that had accompanied her former years spent in Florence as a scribe for the Church.

The slight scratching sound of words being placed on paper began to fill her senses, each pen mark resounding in intensity from each book lining the walls around her.

"All these souls," she said. "All the ones I know are writing their stories as we speak."

"Of that they are," George replied as the noise soon abated having reached its goal of attention. "Now," he motioned to the pen before her fingertips, "it is time for you to join them."

His words were all it took for her reach for the pen and so lean over her book, it's blank pages inviting what was to be transcribed across them.

George watched her write, as did his view follow her strides across the library as predicted, her focus cast over numerous books of another's tale.

To and thro she would leave the table, her frowns increasing the intensity of her search for the pages that would provide the key for her own interlinking of character, location and ultimate lesson housed within chosen soul's liaison with her own.

Instinctively she knew of the lessons she must learn and so with dexterity and delicate prose weaved said trials within her own teaching to others, every paragraph completed a complex mingle of emotion and sentiment designed to stimulate the mind and wits of all concerned.

Time mattered little in the library halls that now saw to such tenacity of spirit, with George looking up occasionally to the windows above them. He soon lost count in watching yet another dawn form, become lost in a daylight that soon succumbed to nightfall only to be replaced by another approaching day.

In patience he stayed his ground, aware of his calming presence beside the soul who wrote with admired ferocity and verve.

Soon came the time he awaited.

"This is where you come and get me," she said, her view still held on the book at her fingertips.

George continued his wait until she at last raised her head from her vocation and looked to him.

"Finished," she said, placing the pen down beside her completed new life story.

"Good," George glanced down to the book that now contained all that was needed for the next step to come. "Now it is time for you to live that which you have written."

She knew this moment would come and without a word closed her book, placed it atop her loved one's that had never left her side in all the time she had composed her next life story and carried them both to where she had found them.

Standing back and looking to them sat side by side in gentle glow on one of the library's many shelves she smiled to both volumes before returning to George who now stood before the doorway in which they had entered the vast library.

"Now you are ready," he said as she joined his side.

"I am," she whispered as both walked out into the dawn's sunlight hours.

Stepping out into the subtle warmth of dawn's early stride, they left the library that had revealed so much and walked to the cliff edge. Looking to a horizon of colour, reds and purples gave way for a domineering orange glimmer, preparing for daylight to begin its governance of blue.

The seas also displayed the luminescence of each changing hue and tone, the white crescents of wave and surf catching an eternal cycle of differing shades as they formed and faded across calm waters.

Lost in the splendour of such a sight, the one who now held great understanding of times passed and of the one to come turned to George.

"Thank you," she said to him.

"Of this there is no need," George smiled to her. "All you have learnt and experienced within those library walls was there all the time."

"Within me," she said, her awareness that the knowledge accumulated in all the lifetimes she had lived had never left her.

"All the tools needed are there, all the answers to the trials met with in each lifetime are within you, all you have to do is search deep inside your heart to find them and so aid whatever difficulty or problem that may confront you in the present."

"Because I have met and overcome a similar situation in my past," she spoke with enhanced understanding, the solutions to life's sometimes hardships encountered reaching fruition.

"And so shall you continue to do so in each lifetime," George turned his view back onto the seascape vista before them. "The vast waters into which a soul dives as it takes on a new lifetime, a new journey, is filled to the brim with the answers sought towards finding happiness and contentment. Each wave, be it gentle or fierce, carries the answers and solutions to what is needed for advancement and conquer of all within the arena of life."

As George fell silent she joined his view ahead. The dawn before them began to recede as the faint yellow that had replaced orange tinges faded into a veneer of white awaiting its dashes and swathes of blue sky.

With her awareness to resolutions met with in living one lifetime after another a new concept came to her.

"There is nothing to fear," she said, her tone as soft as the early morning breezes finding a way across her cheek.

"And why?"

"Because there is no death," she became lost in her discovery, her heart lightening on such realisations.

"Now you see," George looked to her, his wait for her conclusion at last met with. "How can a soul hold any fear towards dying when the truth of the matter is that the soul never dies, as has been shown within the library of knowledge each and every soul has also."

"The soul continues forwards on each occasion," she said, her voice a whisper once more.

"The essence of which carries all the traits and characteristics that makes all souls unique, and so, in the realisation that another life awaits that is often filled with those we love and who love us too, any fear vanishes from the mind and heart of those it once encapsulated."

Knowing all the answers she would ever need were at hand within her own heart and that her soul always continues onwards, the lightness she had experienced before expanded into more.

"What's happening?" She asked George, her questioning concealing no fear at all.

"Look," he turned and pointed behind them.

The bush that had greeted their arrival after a steady climb from beach to cliff top gave a slight glow as both looked to it.

The flowers that had blossomed before her eyes in prelude to entering the library were gone.

"As with all lived and experienced in each lifetime," George said. "Those petals are but distant memories, each delicate moment blown away on the winds of time."

"And now?" She looked to the twisting maze of branch and stick.

"This is of your design. All you wrote of in that new chapter has been incorporated into what we see before us now. These twisting and turning pathways portrayed in your new lifetime to come are waiting to flower, waiting to be seen, as are the surrounding thicket of life stories of those you will meet with on your new journey. Those whose hearts you will touch as they too shall touch yours also."

The lightness she had felt returned and she looked to George for reassurance once again.

"I am at your side," he told her. "Now it is time for another journey."

George's words pulled on distant memories of times long ago, prompting her to reach for his hand.

"Will I remember?" She asked, her fingers curling around his.

His smile gave her the answer she knew was to come.

"A little. Sometimes you shall recall moments that seem familiar to you. Some locations will carry the memories of times spent there, as will the eyes of others hold a similar resonance, echoes of connections made through the centuries, each link holding the identification of a treasured warmth so strong it carries with you from one lifetime to another."

Comfort came in the knowledge given now, an awareness that all important to her own soul's advancement and that of others would appear, and although she knew those appearances of recollections passed would be fleeting, they would be enough for her wellbeing, her heart and her own unique life story.

"And you will be there too," she smiled, her eyes wide in the naïve essence wrapping around her now, preparing her for the new life she had written only moments earlier.

"Every step of the way," George told her, his hand giving a gentle squeeze around hers.

Turning back to the waters ebbing and flowing across white sands she gasped to the sight.

"What a view," she said, as if seeing it for the first time. She looked to George and then to the library. "Who lives there?"

George smiled to her once more. It was always this way. With all the trials and tribulations he would accompany the soul now stood at his side through, the moments he met with now were always a joy to him.

"Where am I? It's beautiful," she said, her curiosity shining through her gradual forgetting of all that had gone before, so signalling she was ready to continue, to act out the lifetime her soul had sculptured and laboured over within the library she now retained no knowledge of.

"Look," George motioned back to tranquill waters lit by the bluest of blue skies.

Glancing to George in awe, making sure he too witnessed such a sight, she looked to the where sky met with water and to the white light that began to form across its horizon.

Her hand still held tight in George's, she looked to the beach wondering if she would one day walk upon it before peering up to the sky.

Another gasp came from her as she made out the faint sparkle of distant stars still evident in morning's early beginnings.

George watched her raise her hand and trail a fingertip across the fading line of galaxies dissecting the sky in two, much the same way he had done so on each occasion, be it that of ancient man in search for a new home for his family, crusading knight, a Florentine monk, artist's model, amid the solitude of an artist of Japan and of France also, through the eyes of a child surrounded by the warfare of others, or in the shadows of the Himalaya mountain range.

Sure he would soon be watching the soul beside him trace a finger over such cosmic displays again he smiled.

"Now you are ready," he said as pure white light encompassed them both.

.

EPILOGUE

Midtown Manhattan
New York City, USA
2089AD

Walking across polished tiles, remembrances of a lifetime visiting the hallways and many rooms of New York's finest gallery came to her.

Since a child she had accompanied her father on her exploration of the paintings held within its grand walls, his delight towards the works of art displayed instilling her young mind with matched enthusiasm.

In her now solitary strides she gave a smile to such memories, recalling how with her hand in his she had watched his white beard raise and fall in reply to his joyful expressions of masters old and new.

Those times had passed long ago and now over four decades later it was she who took the mantle, her own pleasure equalling the one who had introduced her to such beauty represented in the artistic pursuits of humankind's soul.

Continuing onwards towards her goal, her thoughts returned to the painting she longed to see, the one that had pulled on her senses since her first view upon the portrait displayed across its wooden canvas, her hand held tight by the father who had always shown such kindness to her.

It was always considered that she herself would pursue a life in the arts. Teenage years fuelled by a want to produce artworks that rivalled the ones that surrounded her walk now were almost reached, yet a change of heart had come to her then in a calling into the medical world.

It caused no pain to leave the oil paints and canvases which had always held her fascination. The passion she had shown to learn the ways of healing the sick had resembled that of artistic endeavours, and so she surmounted to a life amongst those in need of healing and good health.

Without a need for directions her first call happened upon the chambers displaying the Asian artworks which had always enticed her attention.

Pausing for a moment, she looked to the small brass plaque mounted beside the entrance. Reading to who the room was dedicated she saddened to the story of the one whose name was displayed in engraved lettering, recalling the story of how the life of the young woman who saw to the restoration of the artworks within had come to a close, and of the talent she had loving displayed on bringing canvases of old back to the vivid colours of their original conception.

This caused her to consider the life she led now. In all her experience of healing those whose bodies had failed them there had been one overriding feature which had over the years become instilled within her with each malady and disorder encountered.

The sanctity of life had proved the defining matter of her being. Having seen so much pain and discomfort in others, both in her own homelands and that of the far reaches of the world, her understanding as to the fortune of being of sound health had been enhanced and was something she knew she would never take for granted.

Another perception which led on from such insights had come to her in her days of treating others. No matter where she had been, be it the poverty stricken parched lands of Africa or the far reaches of Asian climes, she had watched those of little give to those of similar standing, and so bringing forward the appreciation that kindness was indeed endemic within the heart of humankind. An insight that aided her in her continuation of helping others, her faith restored in the prevalence of compassion and understanding given by others to the weak and of these in need.

With these familiar thoughts filling her heart she reached out and trailed a finger across the young woman's name who had passed over half a century ago, sentiments of kinship towards her appearing in the love she was aware each shared towards the innovations of artists throughout history.

Entering into the silence between those displays of oil and lacquer she took a seat before the piece which had given her delight since she could remember.

She knew the piece well. Having studied it composition over the years it never surprised her that there would always be something new to see within its opus of the human condition, created by one who adhered to the wants of peaceful philosophies.

Flowing over the portrayal of tranquill waters at its base, her view ran over the deity at its centre and the myriad of life surrounding such serenity before reaching the blue skies and its lone bluebird, still yet alive in flight.

It was this creature that had caught her imagination on her first visit to the room in which she now sat, her wonder to the vision of calmness no different now as to then.

Aware of the time and her need to return to an afternoon of appointments, she stood and left the Tibetan masterpiece behind, pausing briefly to smile to the unfinished Japanese representation of a solo swimming koi carp, the one she would always hound her father for answers as to why its fins and scales were missing.

Onwards in her quest to meet with the pensive stares of half a millennia ago her pace slowed on passing the tall canvas on loan from its European home, the artwork she knew well from her younger studies in books and photographs, the work of Spanish hand that had given the art world a much needed thrust into the modern ideals and concepts of the twentieth century.

So too did the piece cause an appeal to her soul, its allure found in the stance of abstracted dancers, lean of poise and bearing.

Her pace quickened on leaving all these treasures behind her. The familiar aching within her to reach her chosen painting grew stronger on her advance, although another ache came to her in these moments, one which had grown over the preceding few years to her surprise.

With a successful career in hospitals throughout the world she had opted to return to the city of her birth, a decision it seemed that had been influenced by the gallery through which she now marched.

There had although been another factor which had raised its head. A surprise to herself and others who knew of her feisty temperament and more so the solitude she had always adored. For the first time it seemed she wanted to share that solitary gait of which she was recognised to hold so dearly. The want of another had never been an aspect in her life before.

As with her departure from cherished artworks of her past, she too left thoughts of the heart behind on nearing the one she had come to see.

Stopping before the small dimly lit gallery she waited for the three people allowed at one time to view what lay within, a private hope that she would be able to stand alone with the painting. Within minutes her wish was granted and she stepped into the low lighting of her delight.

Silence fell over her as she held her breath to the sight before her. Looking to the fine brush marks portraying slight curl of hair her view fell to the delicate cheekbones those locks framed, her heart focused on the pensive stares of renaissance beauty.

Often she would wonder of the thoughts of the woman presented to her. Imagining herself standing within the studio watching artist and model in silent ambiance, she considered if the young woman before her worried if her exquisite looks would one day fade in the passing of time's fire.

Becoming wrapped up in the splendour of an old master's skills she did not hear the footsteps of another enter the gallery behind her.

"She looks familiar," the new visitor said in soft tones.

On any other occasion she would have been startled by the unknown presence of another, yet she felt no fear in hearing those words. Her soul somehow knew from whom they came.

"She does?" She replied, her view not leaving the painting as the man took a place beside her.

"Yes," he spoke once more. "She looks like you."

Not knowing whether to be flattered for the beauty before her or to hold some embarrassment that maybe she too shared such preoccupied stares, she left the woman of browns and ochre and turned to the owner of the voice beside her.

She caught her breath within the confines of the gallery once more.

"I suppose she does," she smiled to him, becoming lost within the green eyes that greeted her and the golden flecks that danced within them.

The End

THE GEISHA AND THE MONK

Two souls born thousands of miles apart.
Together each shall follow a similar path

A novel
Julian Bound

Japan, 1876
A girl is born, her life path to be the famed Geisha she is destined to be.

Tibet, 1876
A boy is born, ordained to be the revered Lama of which he is recognised.

San Francisco, 1900
At the dawning of a new century fate brings them together,
a lifetime away from all they have ever known.

The Geisha and The Monk is a story of love and compassion, holding many answers to life's questions which are explained through Buddhist teachings.

As well as sharing an insight into the preparation and lifestyle of a Geisha, 'The Geisha and The Monk' explores the seldom known life and training of a Tibetan novice Buddhist monk within the monasteries of Tibet.

SUBWAY OF LIGHT

Sometimes a second chance is all we need.

A novel
Julian Bound

No one can tread your path but you, yet we should never
dismiss those who join us on our journey from time to time.

Following an accident, Josh finds himself sat alone at the back of an empty
New York subway car on a deserted station, his memory gone and with no
recollection of how he arrived there.

A man approaches and introduces himself as George. George tells Josh he
has been taken out of his life to partake on a journey on the train. Acting as
a guide, George explains their train will make several stops and that each
station they visit may begin to seem familiar to him.

Arriving at their first stop, Josh and George witness a young couple meet
for the first time. George tells Josh that the young couple are soul mates
rediscovering one another again.

The ensuing stations Josh and George's subway train stops at follows the
young couple's life through the years as they experience courtship, marriage,
tragedy and happiness.

In watching their lives unfold, Josh gradually begins to gain awareness
through George's guidance, until, as his memory starts to return, it is Josh
himself who must decide the fate of his own final destination.

'Subway of Light' is a healing book of love found, lost, and regained
through the act of belief and trust, not only within ourselves but in others.
The story of one man's awakening, 'Subway of Light' is a heartwarming
modern day tale of kindness and understanding.

LIFE'S HEART ETERNAL

One man's journey through the centuries

A novel
Julian Bound

'My name is Franc Barbour. I was born on the 20th July 1845 in the town of Saumur, deep in the heart of the Loire Valley, France. The truth of the matter is I simply never died.'

These are the opening words a young nurse reads in an old leather bound journal given to her by a stranger. She soon uncovers the story of one man's journey through the centuries.

Following Franc's path from 1845 until present day, 'Life's Heart Eternal' is a tale of how our actions in each lifetime often hold consequences in the next.

With Franc's travels across the world in his endless years, the reader anticipates his next encounter with those reincarnated from his past and of what lessons each shall meet with.

'For who has never wondered what it would be like to live forever?
'

THE SOUL WITHIN

Because everyone longs for
their soul to be touched

A novel
Julian Bound

In releasing our thoughts towards a lifetime imagined,
only then may we have the life our soul awaits.

Falling ill in his home town of Puri on India's eastern coastline, a boy is visited by his spirit guide. Taking him on a journey around a tranquil lake, together they observe those living along its banks.

As his guide explains the life lessons they encounter through her subtle teachings, the boy's emerging awareness to matters of the soul leads him to discover the reasons behind their meeting as his story unfolds.

A heartening tale of awareness, 'The Soul Within' offers its readers an insight into another's awakening, guided by the love and kindness held within us all.

THE SEVEN DEADLY SINS AND THE SEVEN HEAVENLY VIRTUES

As viewed in religion, ancient mythology and art and literature

Julian Bound

The Seven Deadly Sins and the antidotes of the Seven Heavenly Virtues have been depicted throughout history in forms of both Greek and Roman mythology and in the world of art and literature.

Perceived as being associated within the doctrine of the Christian faith, the eastern religions of Buddhism, Hinduism and Sikhism all share a parallel view of the seven sins and virtues, yet are expressed in the theology of different precepts.

'The Seven Deadly Sins and The Seven Heavenly Virtues' examines the similarities of each sin and virtue within religions of the world, and of the portrayal in mythology and art and literature.

'The Seven Deadly Sins and The Seven Heavenly Virtues' also invites the reader to identify which sin they are prone to and of what virtue best displays their greatest qualities; the result of which is an exploration of the self within the aspects of the seven sins and seven virtues, and so acting as a guide for each soul's unique individual path.

POETRY

HAIKU

Japanese Poetry

Julian Bound

Using the traditional Japanese form of Haiku poetry written to evoke a thought or emotion within its unique simplicity of creation. Following the four key elements of self, each poem and accompanying photograph are presented to the reader for contemplation of both the physical and metaphysical world around them.

Of Nature
The foundations of all life, beauty glimpsed to enhance the inner self.

Of Mind
The primary strides towards an awareness of being, the first true steps taken.

Of Love
The practice of awareness, the deepness of the self transformed into action, not only for another but for the self, the foundations of the pillars of all happenings.

Of Being
The apex of perception. The act of living a life filled with and emitting love.

Of Calmness
The tranquillity of finding stillness of mind and being, brought forward in the awareness of nature and love for all.

TEARDROPS OF ASIA

An Anthology of Poems

Julian Bound

JAPAN

NEPAL

TIBET

INDIA

BHUTAN

THAILAND

CAMBODIA

INDONESIA

MYANMAR

CHINA

An anthology of Japanese Haiku and traditional poetry influenced by the author's nine year journey through Asia and South East Asia.

Drawing on the sights, sounds and emotions of a continent filled with such rich diversity of life, traditions and cultures, 'Teardrops of Asia' examines the unified depths of the differing qualities of each country, from the tranquill Japanese gardens of Kyoto, to the barren landscapes of southern Tibet, the riverside temples of northern Cambodia and the remote monastery fortresses of central Bhutan.

THE MIDDLE WAY

Photography and Words

Julian Bound

A 6,331mile/10,156km photographic journey through seven Buddhist countries in seven months. Documenting the life, traditions and culture of Buddhism in India, Nepal, Bhutan, Myanmar, Thailand and Cambodia.

From Dharamshala, India's 'Little Lhasa', to a gathering of 5,000 Buddhist monks and nuns in Lumbini, Nepal, the birth place of Buddha, then onwards through the secluded Kingdom of Bhutan, the high altitudes of Tibet's remote monasteries, the golden temples of Myanmar and Thailand and the riverside shrines of Cambodia.

Travelling through altitudes of 16,900 feet /5,150 meters to sea level, and between temperatures ranging from -18 to 38 degrees, a journey of discovery on the path of the middle way.

TIBET

Photography and Words

Julian Bound

With over 100 photographs in colour and black and white.

A photographic journey through Tibet's villages, landscapes, towns and the capital city of Lhasa.

From the Tibetan Everest base camp to the world's highest mountain pass of Ganchula and the 14,570feet/4,441m high Yamdrok Lake with its vast collection of multi-coloured prayer flags.

Passing through the snowcapped peaks of the Himalaya mountain range and onwards to the monasteries and temples of Drepung and Sera of Lhasa, and Jokhang Temple of Barkhor Square in the heart of the Tibetan capital.

PHOTOGRAPHY BOOKS

TIBETAN
TOKYO, THE BIG MIKON
JAPAN, LAND OF THE RISING SUN
GEOGRAPHIC: 100 PHOTOGRAPHS
TOKYO FROM THE HIP
ASIA FROM THE HIP
A DESIGN FOR LIFE
PORTRAITS OF NEPAL
JETHAL VILLAGE OF RECOVERY
KATHMANDU FROM THE HIP
SIEM REAP FROM THE HIP LUANG
PRABANG FROM THE HIP
BANGKOK FROM THE HIP
DOCUMENTING ASIA VOLUMES 1 – 9
IN THE BUDDHA'S IMAGE
TEMPLES OF NORTHERN ASIA
TEMPLES OF SOUTH EAST ASIA
HOW TO BE A TRAVEL PHOTOGRAPHER
HOW TO BE A DOCUMENTARYPHOTOGRAPHER
HOW TO BE A STREET PHOTOGRAPHER
IN THE FOOTSTEPS OF BUDDHA EYE
OF THE BEHOLDER
FURTHER JOURNEYS
JOURNEYS
TIBET
THE MIDDLE WAY
PORTRAITS OF ASIA
THE PEOPLE OF NEPAL
RELIGIONS OF INDIA
EARTHQUAKE NEPA
INDONESIA
GYUTO
A PORTUGUESE LEGACY
A WALK AROUND THE BLOCK IN...

21994405R00113

Printed in Great Britain
by Amazon